John's Journey

Paul Hodgson

Dedication

For my wife Jennifer, who is my soul mate and best friend.

Table of Contents

Part II

Foreword by Bill Fellows

I first met Paul back in 2005 when the people producing the film based on his life, 'Give Them Wings' (then called 'Darlo 'til I Die'), approached me about playing his father, Norman. He struck me that day as a very determined person, and this has proved to be the case many times throughout our friendship, which continues to this day.

Unfortunately, for one reason or another, the original Producers were not able to get the project off the ground. Although we had kept in touch, it was not until 2007 that I met him and his friend, Ian Carter, at the Cannes Film Festival. At one of our many catch-ups, they told me that the producer they now had on board 'had the money in the bag' and that they were 'To treat this trip to Cannes as a holiday'. This turned out to be totally untrue, and worse was to follow for Paul when the producer tried to steal his story, which heralded the beginning of a three-and-a-half-year legal battle that ended up being heard at the Patents Court in London back in 2011.

Although Paul and his team won the case, they emerged from the courtroom with a blank piece of paper, as they were not allowed to use any of the material that had been presented as evidence in the court case.

Many people would have given up after this, but not Paul. He and a couple of others set about writing a new script, and around this time, I was asked to join the team as an advisor. I was extremely pleased to do this.

I introduced them to local film director Dan Perry and casting director Sam Claypole. Within six months, we had the cast to shoot a trailer for the film over two weekends. Several well-known film and TV actors featured in it, including Mark Stobbart ('Just Married' and 'Harrigan' James Baxter ('Still Open All Hours'), and Tracy Wilkinson ('Bad Girls' and 'Billy Elliot'). And yes, I did get to play 'Norman'.

Despite the trailer's initial success, little did we know at the time that it would take a further eight years for Paul and his team to finally raise the money to shoot the film. In between, he was involved in a serious car accident that almost cost him his life. In my honest opinion, it is incredible that he recovered sufficiently (I know he still faces problems related to it to this day) to coordinate the raising of the funds, write most of the script, and coproduce the film.

I still remember the phone call as if it were yesterday when Paul said, 'Bill, we have got the money together to make the film'. I can remember thinking,' Good on yer son'.

No one was prouder than I when I walked on set for the first time, as I knew exactly what Paul had gone through to make his dream a reality. Even in 2025, it is out there for everyone to see. Not bad for someone who had no training whatsoever in the film business. For that, I take my hat off to him. Not many people in that position have achieved that, and he should be proud of himself. I have spoken to him about this, and he does not come across that way at all. In his mind, he set himself a target (completing and distributing the film), achieved it, and then moved on to his next project.

It only leaves me to wish Paul all the best with this, his first-ever novel. If it ever makes it to the big screen, I have been promised the role of 'Peter'; if this happens, it will be a pleasure to work with this guy again.

All the very best, my friend!

Bill Fellows

PART I

Preface

The year is 1912, and several students rush in different directions on the Cambridge University campus to reach the results board.

John Wray is carrying his books under his arm while trying (with great difficulty) to negotiate the throng. Amongst the sheer number of people, he spots his friend Hans Eckhart and quickly heads towards him.

Once he is close enough to him, he taps him on the shoulder. 'Hello, Hans. It will take ages to get close enough to see the board. I will come back when it's quieter, as it's pointless at the moment. I was wondering if you fancy a beer tonight? Hopefully, we can both celebrate getting our degrees together'. Hans nods. 'Yeah, I agree. I am coming back at lunchtime too. Do you fancy meeting then and getting our results? John smiles. We can also firm up our plans to go to the pub. 'Good idea. I will see you back here at lunchtime'. The German nods. John briefly touches his hand as they part.

The pair are sitting at a table in the crowded pub that evening. In front of them are several empty glasses. John looks at his friend. 'I cannot believe we have completed our courses. We will have our degrees in our hands very soon; you will be in history, and I will be in German and other

languages. He nods. 'It is a far cry from when we first met on our very first day at Cambridge …'

John's room door is open as he unpacks his things. He spots Hans entering the room next door, carrying a large suitcase. He looks at him with a smile on his face. 'You must be John, my new neighbor?' John stops what he is doing and turns towards him. He smiles back at his fellow student, who stares at him for just a bit too long. John notices and blushes slightly before composing himself. He glances at the man in front of him and asks, 'Hans?' The German nods. John goes out into the corridor and shakes his newfound friend's hand as he continues. 'Good to meet you, Hans'. His neighbor smiles and then replies. 'I am very pleased to meet you too'.

Returning to the pub, John smiles. 'Yes, I agree; we have certainly both come a long way since that first day here at Cambridge. It seems like a lifetime ago now that I think about it'.

Chapter One

It is now five years later, and Private John Wray is one of several British soldiers marching towards the front in France. At the head of the group are an officer and a sergeant. The officer glances at him. 'Sergeant, can you go and get Private Wray to come and join me?' The sergeant salutes him. 'Yes, Sir.' He then turns and quickly heads down the line.

Within five minutes, John joins the officer. 'You wanted me, Sir?' He quickly glances at him. 'Yes, private. I have been thinking, and I would like you to be my runner if and when I need to send urgent messages to and from HQ. I know you are reliable because I have read your file and, indeed, have spoken to many people about you. Not one of them said a single bad thing about you'. He smiles. 'That is good to hear. Yes, Sir. I would be honored. Thank you very much for thinking of me'. The officer then looks at John's leg. 'By the way, is that back to normal now, Private Wray?' He nods. 'Yes, Sir, it is fine; thanks to Doctor Smith; he did an absolutely fantastic job'. The officer looks at him. 'Who is he?' 'He is the Doctor who saved my leg. If it were not for him, I would not be here now, Sir, as I would no doubt have had a wooden leg and would be living a completely different life'. The officer shrugs his shoulders. 'That is very good to

hear, private. You can rejoin the men now'.
Without saying anything else, John salutes him and
then heads back down the line.

Two weeks later, the British trench is under
heavy German bombardment. Shells are exploding
everywhere. All the soldiers are hiding wherever
they can to avoid being hit.

Like his comrades, John is hunched in a
corner in an attempt to avoid being killed by the
incoming shrapnel. The sergeant joins him and
glances in his direction. 'The top man wants to see
you straight away, private'. He nods. 'Yes, Sir. I
will make my way there now'. He gets up, salutes
the sergeant, and heads towards the officer's
quarters.

Five minutes later, John enters the officers'
quarters. He is sitting at the table with a half-full
cup of tea in front of him, reading a map. John
salutes him. 'You sent for me, Sir?' The officer
looks up, and from his desk, he hands him a letter.
'Yes, I did, private. As soon as possible, I would
like you to deliver this letter to General Robinson
at Headquarters; please do not deliver it to anyone
else, but only to him. Then wait and bring his reply
back to me as quickly as possible. I want to
emphasize that time is of the essence. He nods and
then salutes the officer, 'Yes, Sir. I will do'. The
officer briefly pauses and glances at him. 'On
second thoughts, private, take two men with you. It

is vitally important that the letter reaches
Headquarters by any means possible. With this in
mind, I am now of the opinion that three men will

give us a much better chance of getting through
than one. The sergeant will pick two men for you'.
He nods. 'Yes, Sir, I agree. I will let the sergeant
know'. He salutes the officer again and then leaves.

Back in the trench, John once again dodges
the incoming shells as he walks slowly along,
avoiding explosions and several injured men
throughout his perilous journey. Five minutes after
leaving the officer's quarters, he comes across the
sergeant. He salutes him and then shows him the
letter. 'Sir, the commanding officer wants me to
take two men with me to deliver this to
Headquarters. He said that you would pick them'.
The sergeant glances at the letter before John puts
it into his top pocket. He then looks around and
spots two soldiers crouched down, attempting to
avoid the incoming artillery fire. The sergeant
looks at the pair and then shouts, 'Privates White
and Walsh, hurry up and get your gear ready. You
are going with Private Wray. He will fill you both
in on the details. Both soldiers salute him before
gathering their supplies. The sergeant then looks at
John. 'Wray, you are in command. What you say
goes. I will let Privates White and Walsh know the
situation. He nods and then salutes before shouting,

'Yes, Sir. Thank you, Sir'. The sergeant glances at him. 'Go and get your gear ready, soldier'. He then shouts, 'Yes, Sir'. Finally, he salutes him and then carefully but quickly heads back up the trench towards where his own gear is stored.

Chapter Two

Forty-five minutes later, John, Privates White and Walsh are running towards the British Headquarters. Private Walsh glances at John. 'I wonder what is in the letter that is so important? I mean, it is very rare for three runners to be sent to deliver one letter'. He shrugs his shoulders. 'I do not know, Private Walsh. As long as one of us gets it there, that is all that matters. That said, I got the impression from the commanding officer that it is crucial'. The private nods without saying another word.

As John and his comrades continue their journey, Private Walsh glances at John. 'If you do not mind, can I ask you a question?' He smiles and then nods. 'Yes. Of course, you can private'. Private Walsh smirks. 'I have often wondered something about you. You have got a posh voice. How come you are not an officer instead of a private?' He smiles. 'It all started with a conversation I had with my father. Let me explain:

I was sitting at our kitchen table reading a newspaper in July 1914. I remember the headline as if it were yesterday, 'Great Britain declares war on Germany'. I still remember the Prime Minister's speech. It went something like this 'Great Britain is

in a state of war with Germany. It was officially stated at the Foreign
Office last night that Great Britain declared war

against Germany at 7 pm. The British Ambassador in Berlin has been handed his passport.

War was Germany's reply to our request that she should respect the neutrality of Belgium, whose territories we were bound in honor and by treaty obligations to maintain inviolate.

Speaking in a crowded and hushed House yesterday afternoon, the Premier made the following statement: 'We have made a request to the German Government that we shall have a satisfactory assurance as to the Belgian neutrality before midnight tonight.'

The German reply to our request, officially stated last night, was unsatisfactory'.

That aside, this is roughly how our conversation went.

'I am going to volunteer. It is something I feel I have to do. Hans will probably be conscripted by the German government. I just hope we both get through this bloody war unscathed.' My father paused for several seconds. 'Don't you think like that, son. I am sure that you will both get through this unscathed'. I can remember smiling. 'I miss his company. We are very close'. He nodded. 'I know you are. You will see him again when this is all over, though'. I was not as confident as my father, so I simply said, 'I sincerely hope so'. My father quickly glanced at me before saying, 'You know, John, you could get into the army as an officer'. I shook my head and said, 'That is not for me. I want to go in as a private'.

Later, I was offered a commission, but I turned it down because I did not want to be an officer.

Returning to the present, Private Walsh smiles, glances at John with a look of surprise on his face. 'I cannot believe that you remembered the Prime Minister's speech! Unbelievable! So, that aside, did you do all the training we had to do?' He nods. 'Regarding the speech, it just stuck in my head for some reason. I honestly do not know why. And, yes. Of course, I did the same training as you two. Let me explain …'

A few days after his conversation with his father, John stands in the Army Examination Room. A sergeant is standing beside him. He points to a board in front of John. 'Can you read the letters on the bottom row?' He nods. 'N, E, H, D, L, T, O and A'. The sergeant grins, then points towards the Height Ruler. 'Your eyesight is fine. Can you go and stand under the Height Ruler over there?' He does as he is asked. He measures his height. 'You are well over the regulation 5:6'. Looking puzzled, John asks, 'I thought the minimum height was 5:3?' He shakes his head. 'No, it has been changed to 5:6'. John nods but adds nothing else to the conversation.

Shortly after, John stands with a bible in his hand, and the sergeant hands him a card. 'Can you please read what is on the card out loud?' John nods before starting to read, 'I, John Wray, do make Oath that will be faithful and bear true Allegiance to His Majesty King George V, His Heirs, and Successors, and that I will, as in duty bound, honestly and faithfully defend His Majesty, His Heirs, and Successors, in Person, Crown and Dignity, against all enemies, and will observe and obey all orders of His Majesty, His Heirs and Successors, and of the Generals and officers set over me. So, help me God'. The sergeant smiles. 'Congratulations, you are now officially in the British Army. Welcome aboard son'. He nods and then salutes the sergeant. 'Thank you, Sir'.

A week later, John is training on the rifle range at the barracks at Catterick Garrison. A different sergeant watches him, together with other soldiers, as they are lying on their stomachs with rifles in their hands. They all shoot their rifles at targets. Most of them miss by some distance. The sergeant shakes his head before yelling, 'Bloody hell. That was absolute rubbish. If you were shooting at Germans, they would all be on top of you by now, and most of you would be dead or, at the very least, badly wounded. Reload and try again, make sure you hit the targets this time. Each of the soldiers follows their sergeant's instructions and shoots again. On this occasion, they all hit their targets. The sergeant smiles. 'That was much better, lads. This time, you killed all the Germans, and more importantly, you are all still alive. Well done'.

The following day, John and the other soldiers carry their full kits on their backs and run through the North Yorkshire countryside. John is at the front of the procession by some distance.

Later, when John is in the barracks, the sergeant approaches his bunk. 'Private Wray, you were one of the fastest finishers I have ever seen on that course. I think you would make an outstanding runner. I will advise the commanding officer that, if possible, he should assign you to that role. Very well done on your performance today, son; it was truly exceptional'. He stands up and salutes the sergeant. 'Thank you, Sir. That means a hell of a lot to me'. He nods and returns the salute before heading towards the door.

A couple of days later, John and several of his comrades return to the barracks for training. On this occasion, they each run at a dummy (one at a

time) with their bayonets. When it is his turn, John
hesitates and then misses it. The sergeant gives him
a dirty look before shouting, 'Do it again, lad.' This
time, he does not stop to think about it at all and
stabs the aforementioned dummy straight in the
heart. The sergeant smiles. 'That is much better,
soldier. A German would not get up from that'.
John salutes him and says, 'Thank you, Sir'.

Back to the present, Private Walsh smirks. 'It
sounds like you had it as hard as I did. In all
honesty, I found it really tough'. John nods. 'Yes,
you are quite correct; it was difficult. Not easy in
the slightest. However, it did prepare me for war,
which is the whole point of it, I suppose'.

Chapter 3

Shortly after, Private White looks at John. 'I have just been thinking, who is Hans?' John smirks. 'So, you speak, Private White, although you are ten minutes behind everyone else. Hans is my friend from Cambridge University'. He gives him a questioning look. 'Is he German?' John nods. indeed, he is. What difference does that make?' The private shrugs his shoulders. 'None whatsoever to me'. John nods without commenting further.

A little later, John looks at Private White. 'Now that you are talking, do you mind if I ask you something?' He nods. 'Yes, no problem at all'. John smiles. 'How come you have a slight Welsh accent and ended up in the North of England?' The private pauses. 'Well, I was born in Wales, just like my coal mining father. When I was ten, we moved to York, where my mother was originally from. The reason for the move was because my Grandma was ill and there was no one to look after her. She had a grocer's shop in the city center, so we all moved into the flat upstairs, and mother and father ran the shop. I must say, I missed living in the Welsh countryside, to be honest. If you'd like, I can tell you more about the events leading up to my family's departure from Wales and their subsequent move to England. It was an interesting time in my life, though, thinking about it now, I did not realize it back then'. John nods, then smiles. 'Yes, that would be interesting to hear if you want to share your story'. He pauses for the second time. 'Of course, I want to. Here goes …'

Ten-year-old Paul White is sitting at the table, finishing his breakfast with his mother, when suddenly there is a loud thump on their front door. Paul continues eating as his mother gets up and leaves the kitchen.

From the kitchen table, he listens to the conversation. He hears his neighbor say, 'There has been an accident at the pit. As far as I know, they are still digging people out.' He then hears the front door slam, and a few seconds later, his distraught mother enters the kitchen and looks at her son. 'Come on. We are going to the pit; there has been an accident.' They both leave without saying another word.

Twenty minutes later, the pair are standing at the entrance to the mine, along with dozens of other people. A middle-aged woman, who is visibly upset, looks at them. 'According to what I have heard, only six men managed to climb out through the choking smoke and dust. They do not expect to find anyone else alive. I have never heard of or seen anything like it in my lifetime, and I have seen the mining here for over fifty years'. She then starts to cry. Paul's mother glances at her. 'Does anyone know who the six men who got out are?' She nods. 'Yes, there is a policeman at the main gate of the mine. He has got the list with the

names of the survivors on it. If I were you, I would
go there'. Paul's mother half-smiles at the woman.
'Thank you very much for your help. Look after
yourself'. She then turns and looks at her son.
'Come on, Paul, let's go'. The pair then head
towards the main gate of the mine.

After fighting through a throng of people,
Paul and his mother arrive at the mine's main gate
within five minutes. At the front of an extremely
long queue, a lone policeman is standing, doing his
utmost to maintain order. Paul's mother grabs her
son's hand and heads towards him.

Eventually, after what seems like a lifetime,
they find themselves standing before him. He looks
sternly. 'You should wait your turn, Mrs.'. She
looks at him. 'Please, have you got the names of
the six men who got out?' 'As I said, you need to
wait your turn, madam'. Paul's mother ignores the
comment. 'His name is Allan White'. He pauses,
not quite believing what he has just heard. 'What
name did you say?' A now-irritated Paul's mother
looks at him and shouts, 'Allan White!' He checks
his sheet and has a shocked look on his face as he
double-checks it again. He hugs her. 'He is one of
the six, young lady. You are the first person to
come to me today, and their family member's name
is on my sheet. Allan is in the Manager's office. I
will let you through straight away'. Paul notices his
mother crying with relief as she looks at the
policeman. 'Thank you so much for your help. I am
truly sorry for snapping at you earlier; it was the

stress of not knowing what was going on. I realize now that you are only doing your job in extremely difficult circumstances, I might add'. He nods, smiles and then lets them through the gate. 'Don't you worry about it. It has been a very stressful day for everyone concerned. By the way, do you know where the Manager's office is?' She shakes her head. 'No. I have never actually been through the gates before'. He smiles. 'That is all right. Come on. I will take you there myself'. He then leads them through the main gate. He ensures that it is closed and locked after they are safely through.

On arrival at the manager's office, the policeman turns to Paul's mother. 'Allan is in there. I really must get back to the main gate now. She holds her hand out. 'That is fine. I can manage from here. Many thanks for your help; it is very much appreciated'. He smiles and then shakes her hand. 'No problem, reuniting you with your husband was brilliant. After dishing out so much bad news to people today, it gave me a massive boost when you came up and told me his name. You cannot ignore the fact that what has happened is horrendous, of that there is no doubt'. With that, he turns and walks back towards the main gate without saying another word.

After composing herself, Paul's mother knocks on the manager's door. Within a few seconds, a podgy balding man opens it, stares at her. 'Yes?' She looks at the man. 'The policeman from the main gate brought me here. He said Allan

White was in here'. The man looks her up and down. 'Who are you?' From inside the office, another male voice shouts, 'Who is at the door, Smithers?' He shouts, 'That is what I am trying to find out, Sir'. Just then, another face appears. The male smiles at her. 'How may we help you, madam?' Paul's mother returns the smile. 'I am Allan White's wife'. She then turns to her son. 'This is his son, Paul. We were told by the policeman at the gate that my husband is here'. The male opens the door. 'Yes, he is. He is shaken up, but otherwise, he is all right. He is just having a cup of tea. Please come in. By the way, I am Mr. Williams, the mine manager.

Paul and his mother enter the office. Sitting on a chair, they see Allan, who is with five other men, who are also sitting on chairs. He looks at his wife, bursts into tears and then blurts out, 'There were twenty of us in the gang that went down the pit today'. He then looks at his five colleagues before continuing, 'Only six of us are left. They have found all the bodies now'. She goes over to her husband and hugs him. 'Come on, let me get you home'. Mr. Williams looks at him. 'It goes without saying that you can have a week off, with full pay, of course'. Allan half-smiles before replying, 'Thank you very much, Sir. That is very kind of you'. He smiles. 'You were a courageous man today, helping to get as many of your workmates out as possible. That took guts. It is the very least I can do for you in return. I have to go and speak to the mine owners and the families of

those who have died now. As you are aware, it has
been an extremely upsetting day for everyone
concerned. If you need anything else before you
go, Smithers will attend to it'. With that, he heads
towards the door.

Before he leaves, he looks at his assistant. 'I
am going to try to find the five remaining men's
family members. If they come down here, ensure
you look after them well. The poor devils are
probably stuck in the queue'. Before he could
reply, Mr. Williams has left the office.

The following week, Paul and his family are
sitting around their kitchen table. Allan looks at his
wife. 'I am due back at the mine in a couple of
days. Apparently, the shaft is now safe to work
down again. So, we must make our minds up one
way or another, whether we are going to York or
not'. She looks at her husband. 'Look, I think this
is a great opportunity for us as a family. Mum
cannot run the shop alone anymore; she said in her
last letter that we could take it over as long as she
can continue to live there and receive a small
proportion of the profits. She also said she could
still do the odd shift if we want to go out'. Allan
smiles at his wife. 'You really want this, don't you
love?' 'Yes, but not only for me; it will be much
better for us all. We nearly lost you last week, and
this opportunity will stop you from ever having to
go down a coal mine again'. He nods in agreement.
'You are right; this is far too good an opportunity to
turn down. I will go and see Mr. Williams later

today and tell him that I am not returning to the mine. We will give a week's notice on the house, and then we can go and start our new life in York'. She excitedly hugs him. 'I had better get writing to my mother then'. She pauses. 'You have made my day; you know that, don't you?' He smiles as he gets up from the table. 'I am glad to hear it, love'.

Returning to the present day, John looks at Private White. 'It sounds like your father had a lucky escape'. He nods in agreement. 'Without doubt, the accident made up his mind that the best thing for our family was to move to York, rather than constantly putting his life at risk by mining in what were hazardous conditions'. John glances at his companion. 'Do you like it there?' He nods. 'Yes, I do now, but it took a bit of getting used to because I, as said earlier, liked the Welsh Countryside. But I now know that my parents did the right thing. Plus, York is a beautiful city. I love the minster. I have been in it many times and can easily spend hours there'. John nods. 'Yes, I agree, York is a nice place. I have been there many times myself. You are quite right about the minster. A few years ago, I spent almost a whole day there. I could not believe how quickly the time passed once I was in there. Without a doubt, it would have been easy to stay there for another couple of hours. I have to say, the whole building totally enchanted me'.

Chapter Four

Shortly after, as they continued their journey, John looked at Private Walsh. 'So come on, private. You have listened to our life stories. What is yours?'

The private pauses for a few seconds. 'I have never told anyone this before, but my mother died suddenly when I was very young. My father was away with the army; if it had not been for my Grandfather, God knows what would have happened to me. Let me explain ...'

John glances at the private. 'If you would rather not tell us, it does not matter in the slightest'. He smiles. 'No. It is about time that I told someone. You two have told me parts of your stories, so it is only right that I do the same'. He then lets out a huge sigh. 'So here goes; it all started when ...'

Eight-year-old Richard Walsh walks around the market in Middlesbrough with his mother, who has a basket on her arm. They occasionally stop at a stall, where she looks at the articles for sale before walking on. Richard looks at his mother. 'I need a new pair of shoes for school, mam. The pair I have got are far too small'. She shakes her head. 'They will have to last you a little bit longer, son. Money is really tight since your dad has been away, and we never seem to receive his pay on time, which certainly doesn't help. If it were not for your Grandfather's help, we would be in the workhouse by now; I am sure of it'. He nods disappointingly'. I understand mam'. Richard's mother struggles to smile at her son. 'Good lad. Anyway, we should get home now; I have to be up for work early in the morning and don't feel very well at all. For some reason, I cannot shake this cold off; it is awful and is not getting any better, no matter what remedies I try'. He looks at her with a concerned expression on his face. 'Can't you just have a day off?' She vehemently shakes her head. 'If I do not go to work, I do not get paid, then I cannot pay the rent, and in some ways more important than that, we also do not eat'. He grabs his mother's hand. 'I know, mam. I was only trying to help because I am worried about you'. She puts her free hand on her son's. 'I know you are son, but honestly, I will be fine'.

Half an hour later, the pair arrive back home. Richard, who has the front door key, takes it from his trouser pocket, opens it, and they both step inside.

Once in the living room, Richard's mother hands him the basket. 'Will you put the shopping away for me, son? I do not feel very well at all, so I am going to bed'. He looks at the clock. 'Mam. It is only four O'clock in the afternoon'. She smiles lovingly at him. 'I know, but I want to be all right for work tomorrow. If I get an early night, I might be able to sleep off whatever is wrong with me.

That is what I am hoping for anyway'. He has a worried look on his face. 'Do you want me to go and get Aunt Jane?' She shakes her head. 'No. I do not want to bother her. She has enough to contend with looking after all her kids to look after without having to worry about me'. He does not push the point. 'All right, mam, as long as you are sure?' She nods, then looks towards the kitchen. 'There is some bread and dripping in the pantry. You can have some of that later if you want. There is some tea left as well, but only one cup because we have to try to make it last until we get your dad's money again'. He nods. 'Do you want anything mam?' She shakes her head. 'No thanks, son. I am off to bed now. I will see you in the morning, love'. She briefly smiles at her son before leaving the room. Richard has a worried look on his face as his mother closes the door. After she has gone, he takes the shopping basket into the kitchen.

The following morning, Richard wakes up with a start. He jumps out of bed, runs down the stairs and notices that the clock on the mantelpiece says 'half past eight'. He then runs back upstairs to his mother's bedroom and knocks on the door. There is no answer. He waits for a few seconds and knocks again. There is still no reply.

He eventually opens the door and notices that his mother is still asleep. He looks at her. 'Come

on, mam. You are late for work'. He pauses,
sensing something is wrong but not quite knowing
what it is or what to do. His mother does not move.

He looks at her once more. 'Mam. Wake up'. There
is still no movement. Slowly, he walks towards his
mother's bed. After taking a deep breath and
stopping himself several times to pluck up the
courage, he eventually touches the 'sleeping'
woman's forehead and immediately notices it is
freezing cold. He screams loudly and quickly pulls
his hand away before running back down the stairs,
taking three at a time in his haste to get out of the
house.

        A tearful Richard runs out of his front door
and up the street towards his Auntie's house. When
he gets there, he hammers on the door with his fist.
Within a few seconds, his Aunt Jane answers.
'Richard, what are you doing here so early, love?'
He wipes his eyes. 'It is me mam. She is not
waking up'. A panicking Jane rushes out of her
house, ignores her open front door, grabs Richard's
hand, and the pair run back down the street.

        Within a minute of the pair entering the
house, Jane looks at her nephew. 'You stay here; I
will go upstairs and check on your mam.' He nods.
'All right, Aunt Jane.' She then runs up the stairs.

        Shortly after, a tearful Jane slowly walks
down the stairs. She stops halfway, looks at her
nephew. 'She is gone, child. There is nothing I can

do'. He briefly looks at his Aunt and then bursts into tears. Once Jane is down the stairs, she hugs her nephew.

A couple of hours later, Richard stands outside his mother's bedroom door, looking through a tiny gap and listens intently as Jane talks to the Doctor, who is also in the bedroom. He hears him say, 'The poor dear died of Consumption'. Jane then reveals, 'We all told her to come and see you, but she wouldn't'. He shakes his head sympathetically. 'In fairness to her, she probably did not have the money to do that as her husband was away, so do not forget that'. She nods, 'Yes, you are right, Doctor'. It must have been very hard for her'. The Doctor glances at her. 'Have you contacted the Undertaker?' 'Yes, I have'. He nods before handing her a document. 'Good, there is the Death Certificate. I am really sorry for your loss'. He heads towards the door, so Richard quickly scampers back into his bedroom.

After the Doctor has gone, Jane and Richard sit at the living room table. Jane looks at her nephew. 'You will have to stay with us until we decide what to do for the best. Your Grandfather is due to arrive from London any day. We will wait until he comes'. He nods. 'All right, Aunt Jane'. She goes into the kitchen and shouts through to Richard. 'We might as well take this food. It would be a shame for it to go to waste'. He is, by now, in a world of his own, quietly sobbing to himself and, therefore, does not hear his Aunt's words correctly.

The following week, Richard sits at the top of the stairs in Jane's house as he listens to the conversation between his Grandfather and his Aunt coming from the living room. He hears her say, 'We are struggling to feed our own kids, never mind an extra one'. His Grandfather nods. 'I fully understand Jane. I am more than happy to take Richard back to London with me until his father returns'. 'Yes, I agree that will probably be the best way forward, both for us and for poor Richard'. His Grandfather then takes some money out of his wallet. 'If it is all right, I will pick him up tomorrow and take him to the hotel where I am staying. Before I forget, here's some money for what you have done for him already. I have also paid the Undertaker, so you do not need to worry about that. We will stay for the funeral; then we will head home afterwards'. Jane eagerly grabs the money and then looks at her Father-in-Law. 'Thanks for that. One final thing: what about the furniture and other things in their house? Some of it will make good money'. Richard's Grandfather gives her a stern look. 'Leave everything as it is. When Christopher comes home, he will not want to find an empty house'. Jane then asks, 'What about the rent?' He reveals, 'I have already spoken to the Landlord and paid him eighteen months' rent in advance, so there will be no problem there. I have a friend who will keep an eye on the place for me, so everything should be all right. I will need your key back so I can give it to him'. She nods and then looks sheepishly at the man in front of her. 'Richard has asked for his mother's wedding ring'.

The middle-aged man gives her a questioning look, 'So, what is the problem? Give it to him'. Jane is now clearly embarrassed. 'I took it off his mother's finger and sold it to a neighbor'. His face changes to one of anger as he cannot believe what he has just heard, and he shouts, 'You did what? Which neighbor? How dare you? It was not yours to sell'. She replies very quietly, 'Mrs. Jones, who lives two doors up'. He then grabs her hand and shouts, 'You had no right to do that. It is theft. Come on, we are going to get it back. Let's hope for your sake that she still has it, because if she hasn't, I'm taking you to the police station. Oh, and by the way, I am taking Richard with me tonight, as you obviously cannot be trusted'.

Back to the present day, John shakes his head. 'Jesus, what a sad story. I am so sorry to hear about your mother'. Private Walsh nods. 'It was a long time ago now, but I still think about her every day'. Private White glances at his comrade. 'Did your Grandfather get your mother's wedding ring back?'. He nods, 'Yes, he did. The neighbor did not want to return it at first, but once he threatened to involve the police, she soon handed it over. Funnily enough, my Aunt Jane pretended she did not have the money to repay the neighbor. My Grandfather then reminded her that he had just given her some money for looking after me. That left her no option but to do the right thing and give her neighbor the money back'. John glances at his companion. 'She sounded like a right one. Anyway, how long did you stay in London?' He smiles.

'Just under a year. Once my Grandfather told my father on his return what had happened, he never spoke to my Aunt Jane again and has not done so since'. He continues. 'We moved back to Middlesbrough, but funnily enough, we rented a different house in a better area. So, I never saw the old place again because my dad picked up our things, which was a shame in a way, as I had many memories from there. However, it was a new start, which is what we both needed. I have to say that I never forgot what my Grandfather did for me when I really needed help. He is quite elderly now, so he lives with my dad, and I see him almost every day, which is really good. As I said, I have never forgotten what he did for me'.

Chapter 5

Twenty minutes later, the three privates continue to run towards their destination. Private Walsh glances at John. 'So, are you into football, John?' He smiles. 'Yes. Sort of. I sometimes go to an odd game with my dad. He is a big Darlington supporter. He hopes they will one day be promoted to the Football League. Though I admit, I am not into it as much as he is'. He nods. 'What league do they play in?' John glances at his fellow private. 'They are in the North Eastern League. In fact, they won it in the 1912/13 season'. He smiles at the memory and then continues. 'He was overjoyed the day they won the title. I will never forget the smile on his face when he came home'. The private grins. 'I can imagine. Who did they beat in their last match?' John shrugs his shoulders. 'You know what, private, I honestly cannot remember 100%. I think that it was Houghton Rovers, but I could be wrong. I did not go for some reason. However, I do recall another occasion when he travelled all the way down to Northampton Town's County Ground during that season for an FA Cup Replay'. In disbelief, Private Walsh shakes his head. 'That was a hell of a long way to travel for a midweek away match. What was the score?' He half smiles. 'They lost 2-0. You are quite right; it was a Thursday night match and, therefore, midweek. He did not get back home until the early hours of the Friday morning. He only got a few hours of sleep before he had to go to work'. His comrade smiles. 'I must say, that is dedication for you. Not many supporters would make that journey for a midweek match. Well done, Mr. Wray; that is all I can say on that subject'. John glances at Private Walsh. 'I will tell him what you said. Who do you support anyway?' He smiles and then divulges, 'Middlesbrough. I think their reserve team play in the same league as Darlington'. John nods. 'Yes, indeed they do. My dad has mentioned them a few times'. He glances at his companion. 'I have never been to Feethams before'. He then smirks. 'I might go there one day to see Middlesbrough Reserves turn Darlington over'. John smiles. 'I think my dad would probably have something to say about that'. He nods. 'I bet he would. Joking apart, I really admire football supporters like your dad. For his sake, I hope they make it into the Football League one day'. 'Thanks, I will tell him that as well'. Private Walsh smiles but does not add to the conversation.

Shortly after, the three soldiers continue their run towards the British Army Headquarters. In the distance, a woman's scream can be heard. Private Walsh stops and looks at his comrades, who also stop running. He glances at John. 'Did you hear that? He nods. 'Yes, I did. Come on, lads, I think we'd better go and take a look and see what's going on over there'. Private White hesitates for a few seconds. 'Shouldn't we ignore everything that might delay us and get straight to headquarters? I mean, by the sounds of it, this letter is critical. 'I agree, but someone might need our help'. Private Walsh looks at them both. 'I am with John on this; I think that we need to go and see what is going on'. John glances at both of his comrades. 'So, we are all agreed?' Both men nod, though Private White is still reluctant. He smiles. 'Fair enough. Come on, lads; let's go'. They then all head in the direction from which they heard the scream.

Chapter Six

The three soldiers head up a long path. After a two-minute walk, they see a farmhouse.

After a further couple of minutes, in a yard near the farmhouse, they spot a German soldier standing near a barn, smoking a cigarette. He is totally unaware of their presence. John glances at Private White. 'As yet, we do not know whether there are any more Germans in the house and, if so, how many. Could you get behind that soldier and either slit his throat or knife him in the back? Then we will try to get into the house'. He nods, 'Yes, no problem at all. I will do whichever is easiest at the time'. Without hesitation, he heads off down the track.

Shortly after, Private White is crouched behind the barn where the German soldier is still standing. He has his bayonet in his hand, gets up, and slowly, step by step, creeps up behind his intended victim.

He continues to creep up behind the soldier with his bayonet still poised. Within thirty seconds, he is directly behind the aforementioned German soldier. He quickly grabs his arms so he cannot move with one hand and then, in one move, slits his throat with the other. As he lets go of his

arms, the already dead German drops to the ground
with blood spurting from his mouth.

After seeing the German soldier fall, John glances at Private Walsh. 'Great. He has done it. Good man! Once he gets back, we will head to the farmhouse. I bet my wages that there will be more Germans in the house'. His comrade nods in agreement, 'I am not betting because I think you will turn out to be right, John'. His cohort grins. 'You are not as daft as you look private'.

A minute later, Private White rejoins his companions. John glances at him, 'Well done for doing that. You made it look easy'. He nods. 'Thanks. I just followed what I learned in training. Slitting his throat was the best way for me to kill him. He did not make a sound'. John remarks, 'In fairness, it does not matter how you do it as long as you get the job done. Anyway, now that that's sorted, come on, you two, let's go and see what's happening inside the house'.

Shortly after, they glance through a window. John shakes his head in disbelief at what he sees and hears through the tiny, open window.

A semi-naked woman in her twenties is lying on the kitchen table.

Her arms are being held down by two German soldiers, one of whom is feeling the woman's bare breasts with his free hand. Meanwhile, a German sergeant is forcibly having sex with her, with his uniform trousers around his ankles, as she is in floods of tears. The soldier, fondling the woman, looks at the sergeant. 'Hurry up. I want my turn'. He smiles and says, 'Do not worry. You will get your turn in good time, private. You look to be having enough fun down there for now anyway'. The soldier looks at the woman's breasts and then smirks. 'Yes, I am, they are nice and firm. But I still cannot wait for my go though. I might give her it up her backside; that will be tighter'. The woman then looks pleadingly at the sergeant. 'Please stop this and do not let him do that to me'. He laughs and then shouts, 'Shut up, you dirty little French whore. This is probably the best sex you have had in years. You will be thanking us later'. The other two soldiers also laugh as they continue holding the woman down.

John looks at his comrades, 'We have to put a stop to this, lads. It is a disgraceful way for anyone to behave'. He then looks at Private Walsh. 'Go and see if any other doors or windows are open. If there is, come back here, and we will all go in together. He nods and then sets off.

A few minutes later, the private returns; he glances at John. 'There is a slightly open side door. We can get into the house that way. It will be tight, but we should be able to get through. John nods. 'Good work, private. Come on, lads, let's put this to an end'.

Shortly after, the three men arrive at the side door, which, as Private Walsh had previously mentioned, is slightly ajar. They all prepare their rifles before squeezing through the gap and into the house.

John and his comrades slowly but surely creep along the passage. Heavy breathing and laughter can be heard as they approach the kitchen door. The three British soldiers head in the direction from which the sounds are coming.

Within a minute, they are outside the kitchen door, which is closed. John pauses for a few seconds, glances at his companions and then whispers, 'I will kick the door open, then I will kill the dirty bastard who is on top of the woman; you two take one of the other two each'. Private Walsh glances at his comrade and again whispers, 'I will take the one on the right of the woman. You take the other'. He nods and then whispers, 'No problem. Let us just get this over and done with'. A couple of seconds later, John kicks the door open.

The threesome enter the kitchen. Before the Germans can do anything to react, there are three loud BANGS, and they are all dead. The sergeant is lying on the floor next to one of his comrades, and one of the remaining soldiers is still lying on top of the clearly shocked woman. John looks at Private Walsh and shouts, 'Get him off her'. Without hesitating, he grabs the dead German by the scruff of his neck and throws him onto the floor. His head crashes against it. Once she is free, John helps the woman to her feet.

A couple of seconds later, John hands the woman her clothes. She half smiles as she puts them on. 'Thank you very much'. He glances at her, 'Are you all right?' She wipes her eyes and then nods, 'Yes, thank you. As well as I can be in the circumstances, and that is down to you three'. He gives her a questioning look, 'So, how did this happen?' The woman pauses for several seconds, then draws a deep breath. 'The four Germans came asking for some milk. When they saw that I was alone, they attacked me'. She then adds, 'The sergeant said that all four of them were going to take me in whatever way they wanted'. John shakes his head in disgust. 'The bastards, I am really sorry, but we have to go soon, as we have to be somewhere else, and we are already behind schedule, but at least they are all dead now. Is there anywhere you can go if anyone comes looking for them?' She shakes her head, 'No. I want to stay here. It is my home'. He looks unconvinced. 'Are you sure?' She nods. 'Yes, I am. I will be a lot more careful next time. That is for certain'. 'Have you got anywhere we can help you to hide the bodies?' Private Walsh smirks and then glances at his fellow private, 'We could feed them to the pigs. There are loads of them out there, and to be honest, that is all they deserve'. John shakes his head. 'I agree in principle, but we have not got the time to cut them up'. The woman glances at John and reveals, 'There is an old cellar in the barn. If you could help me, put them in there, and I will cover the trapdoor with straw. I will then go to my brother's farm. He will come back with me, and we will bury them where no one will ever find them. That would be much quicker for you'. He nods, 'That seems like a good idea. One thing though, where is your husband?' The woman looks at him, 'He is away, fighting the Germans'. John nods, 'What about your brother?' She pauses, 'He was wounded earlier in the war, and he walks with a limp now, so he was told by the army that he could not fight anymore'. He shakes his head, 'It sounds like you have a courageous family. You should be very proud of them'. She smiles, 'I think they are both very brave. We have all done our bit, which is the right thing to do'.

Twenty minutes later, in the barn cellar, John and Private Walsh lay the German sergeant's body next to his three comrades and their rifles. John looks at his helper. 'Well, that is the lot. Come on. We can go now'. His compatriot nods. 'We have done all we can, John, though I still would have liked to feed the bastards to the pigs'. He smirks. 'In an ideal world, so would I, but we do not have the time to do it due to our current circumstances. Anyway, changing the subject, the woman should be all right now until she buries them with the help of her brother'. John half smiles. 'Yes, I think we have done all we can for her. Once they bury them, she will be fine'.

Ten minutes later, John and the other two privates sit at the table, which has been cleaned and reset. John glances at the woman. 'I am sorry, but we really must go'. The woman nods, 'I totally understand'. She then kisses each of the soldiers on the cheek. 'Many thanks for what you did for me today. I will never forget any of you, even if I live to be ninety'. John smiles in the woman's direction, 'No problem at all. I am just glad that we were near enough to hear your scream and, therefore, come to your aid'. She nods but does not add to the conversation. The three soldiers then head towards the back door to continue their journey.

Chapter Seven

The three privates are now heading towards their goal at a breakneck pace. Ten minutes into their journey, Private Walsh glances at John. 'I think that it is terrible what those Germans did to that poor woman. I honestly could not believe my eyes when I first saw what was happening to her'. He pauses for a few seconds. 'Unfortunately, there are good and bad in every race; they were bad at the end of the day'. Private White looks at John, 'They got what they deserved. That is for sure'. He then glances at his fellow private. 'I know that I was not sure about going there and coming away from our mission, but I am glad that we did now'. He smiles. 'In fairness, I could see your point at the time. The letter is critical, but we did the right thing, especially after seeing what they were doing. 'I cannot argue with that'. Private White replies. Private Walsh glances at John a few seconds later and asks, 'Can we stop for a five-minute break soon?' 'Indeed, we can. I think we have earned it after what we have been through today'. He half smiles, 'Yes, it has certainly been different to what I expected; of that there can be no doubt'.

The threesome step off the road and head cross-country in an attempt to find somewhere safe and secluded.

Ten minutes later, John and the other two privates stop walking at a clearing just inside a forest. He glances at his comrades, 'This place will do. We cannot be seen, but unfortunately, we cannot set any fires in case the smoke is spotted'. Private Walsh smirks, 'So, Bully Beef washed down with cold water, it is then'. John smiles. 'You guessed it right, private. It is better than nothing, I suppose'. Each man takes a tin from their pack and starts to open it. John looks at his companions. 'Rather than a five-minute break, we will take fifteen, and then we will need to get moving. We should be able to make up some of the lost time. In my opinion, as long as we reach the headquarters intact, that is all that matters. Both men nod in agreement without saying a word.

After their break time has finished, John looks at his watch. 'Come on, lads. Time is up. We need to get going. Get your gear ready'. Private Walsh smirks. 'No rest for the wicked, I suppose'. John is already on his feet. His two comrades follow suit, and the threesome restart their journey.

Shortly after, John looks at his comrades. 'Give or take, we are about halfway there now. All being well, we should be at headquarters in just over an hour'. Private Walsh nods. 'Considering we helped that woman, we have not done too badly for time'. 'I have just thought she never did tell us her name. I honestly did not think about it until now'. He shrugs his shoulders. 'In the scheme of things, I do not think it really matters. At least we were there to help her when she needed it, which is the main thing'. John nods in agreement, 'Yes, I suppose you are right. I will never forget that incident, though. The private glances at his comrade, 'No, neither will any of us, I suspect'.

A little later, Private White suddenly stops running. John and Private Walsh follow suit. Private White states, 'Sorry for interrupting your conversation, but I thought I heard something'. Private Walsh shakes his head in frustration. 'Oh no. Not again. We will never get to headquarters at this rate if we stop every couple of miles'.

Chapter Eight

In what seems like no time at all, the trio spot two German soldiers in the distance and quickly look for somewhere to hide. John points at a ditch at the edge of the road and shouts, 'Come on, lads, let's get into that ditch over there. Without uttering another word, they all run towards it.

Shortly after, the three men are crouched in the ditch. They hear the soldiers approaching and load their rifles. Once they are in sight, John takes aim, and a few seconds later, there is a loud BANG.

One of the German soldiers is hit in the head. He falls to the ground and is motionless. His comrade does not notice this as he runs past him.

Back in the ditch, Private Walsh glances at John and smiles. 'Got him. Good shot!'

A few yards away, the remaining German quickly fixes his bayonet to his rifle and runs in the direction of the three British soldiers.

Private Walsh takes aim as he sees the soldier heading towards him—his rifle jams. So, Private White does it instead. There is another loud BANG, but he misses the soldier. He then shouts, 'Shit!'

The German soldier then jumps into the ditch

and goes for Private White, stabbing him in the leg with his bayonet in the process. John manages to drag him off his comrade and then hits him with the butt of his rifle. He falls next to Private Walsh.

He then seizes his opportunity and grabs the soldier's rifle before stabbing him in the chest with his own bayonet. Within a few seconds, he is dead.

Instantly, John glances at Private White, who is not fully conscious, then at Private Walsh. 'I will bandage his leg up, then we will need to find somewhere for him to rest up. One of us might have to stay with him whilst the other tries to get through to headquarters. I will decide later what our best option will be, given our circumstances at the time'. Private Walsh nods. 'That sounds like a plan. Whatever you decide, I will be happy with it. On a separate note, I will put the other body into the ditch rather than leaving it on the road. Hopefully, it will be harder to spot'. He replies, 'Good idea private'.

Thirty minutes later, John looks at Private Walsh. 'We will have to carry him. If we find some shelter, we can then decide what to do next. We will have a better idea by then'. He nods in agreement. 'That is fine with me, John'.

They then start their journey with John carrying the wounded Private White on his back.

Chapter Nine

Shortly after, John is still carrying the now unconscious Private White on his back. He glances at Private Walsh. 'I hope he does not lose his leg'. He looks at him with a shocked expression on his face. 'He won't, will he?' John pauses for a few seconds. 'Well, I almost lost mine. It can easily happen'. His comrade gives him a questioning look. 'What happened?' He again pauses for a second or two. 'It all started when I went over the top a couple of years ago. Let me explain ...'

The officer blows his whistle and then leads John and his companions over the top. In no time whatsoever, many of the charging British soldiers are cut down by German machine guns as they race towards the enemy trenches. The officer urges his men on and shouts, 'Come on, lads. Keep going. We are nearly at their trench now'.

As he continues his charge, John is hit in the leg by a bullet. Within another couple of seconds, he is then hit in the arm and falls to the ground. Soldiers trample all over him in their haste to get to the enemy lines as he lies in silence, as gunfire can be heard in the background.

Five hours later, all the gunfire has ceased, and he is now alone, apart from the dead bodies of his former comrades scattered all around him. After thinking for a few seconds, he quietly asks himself, 'Why has no one come to get me by now? It has been ages since the fighting stopped'.

After another few hours, he shakes his head before again saying to himself, 'Well, John, it looks like it is going to be down to you to get yourself back to your trench because it looks as though no one is coming to rescue you'. He then sighs before continuing, 'It is either that or you die here buddy. Then you will be left here with all your dead comrades, probably forever'. He smirks to himself. 'Maybe in 100 years, some farmer will dig up my skull. Now, that is a thought'. He pauses. 'Enough of that silliness; it is time to go'.

After taking a huge breath, he starts to crawl in the direction he came from earlier in the day. In agony, he continues his slow journey back towards the British lines. His trek takes him past many other dead bodies, some of which are either headless or limbless. He does not look at any of them as he continues his painfully slow passage. Suddenly, he hears a moaning sound in the distance, and he slowly approaches to investigate.

A few minutes later, he pauses and says to himself, 'Come on, John, you have to carry on.' He then resumes his slow crawl. The moaning sound grows louder as he continues his snail-like progression towards his short-term goal.

Shortly after, he comes across another wounded soldier. John quickly notices that both of his legs are badly injured. He glances at him. 'What is your name?' The soldier looks weakly at him. 'William'. He smiles. 'Well, William, I am going to try and get you back to our trench, my friend'. He does not reply. John checks that he is still breathing. Once he is satisfied that he is, he slowly starts to drag William's dead weight in the direction of the trench.

Several hours later, a soldier is on guard duty in the British trench. He picks up his periscope and scans the area. He very quickly spots something in the distance and turns to his commanding officer. He shouts, 'Sir, I think I can see something. I am not sure what it is, though.' The commanding officer heads towards him.

Within a few seconds, the commanding officer shoves the soldier out of the way, grabs the periscope, and peers through it. He cannot believe what he is seeing and has an expression of utter amazement on his face. 'My God, it is one of our lads crawling back. He is dragging another soldier along with him. 'Hold your fire men'.

John and William are laid in front of the trench thirty minutes later. The commanding officer looks at two soldiers who are standing next to him and shouts towards them, 'You two, climb over and get them both in here. Hurry up now. We do not want you getting hit by the German snipers'. They do as they are told as the enemy gunfire narrowly misses them.

The pair lift John and then William over the top of the trench to safety. One of them looks at John and asks, 'How the hell did you make it back?' He smiles weakly. 'Only God knows that my friend'.

Returning to the present, Private Walsh glances at John and states, 'That took some guts to drag that William back to your trench'. He shakes his head. 'I did not think about it. I just did what I had to do'. He pauses for a few seconds and then continues. 'I have just thought, I have never told anyone about that incident before'. Private Walsh smiles, 'I feel honored, John. I was wondering, did you ever see William again?' He nods, 'Yes, I did, in the military hospital. Unfortunately, he ended up losing both of his legs'. He glances at his comrade. 'That was a shame. At least he is still alive, I suppose'. John nods as Private Walsh continues. 'You mentioned that you almost lost your leg. If you do not mind me asking, what happened there?' He smiles. 'You ask a lot of questions. But no, I do not mind at all. It was about four weeks after I was discharged from hospital ...'

John is lying in bed. There is a knock at the door. He shouts, 'Come in'. The door opens, and Peter enters. he sits on the side of the bed and quickly notices that John has a worried look on his face. He asks, 'Are you all right, son?' He glances at his father. 'To be honest, I am not sure'. Peter looks concerned. 'What is wrong?' He pauses. 'It is the wound in my left leg. Could you have a look? 'I will get your mother. She will do it. She is better at things like this than me. Knowing my luck, I would probably be sick all over your nice, clean bed. I am sure she would love that'. John smiles and then nods as Peter gets up and quickly heads towards the door.

Harriet (John's mother) enters the room with her husband shortly after. She heads straight over to the bed and carefully pulls the bandage from her son's leg. He winces with pain as she looks at the wound. She then looks up at him with a worried look on her face. 'This wound looks badly infected. We need to get Doctor Smith to come over and have a look at this. He will know for certain, one way or another'. He nods. 'Good idea, mam. It is better to be safe than sorry'.

Doctor Smith enters the room an hour later, with Harriet closely following behind him. He examines the wound on John's leg and then looks at Harriet. 'Yes, you were quite right, it is indeed infected, and quite badly by the looks of it'. They both seem worried as the Doctor looks at his patient. 'I have already checked with the army hospital in case you need to be admitted. Unfortunately, it is full. However, there is room at the one in York'. Harriet shakes her head in frustration. 'There must be something else that can be done?' The Doctor pauses for a second or two and then states, 'We need to act quickly; otherwise, your son will lose his leg; of that, there is no doubt'. John looks at him. 'I cannot do that. I need to get back to the front. I know it's not the best place in the world, but I have to do my bit'. His mother shakes her head in disbelief. 'That should be the last thing on your mind in these circumstances son'. Doctor Smith once again pauses and then glances at them both. 'I have an idea. Let me tell you a story of what happened a few years back when I was an army surgeon in the Boer War'. Harriet gives him a look of frustration. 'What has this got to do with John's leg?' He smiles. 'Be patient, all in good time. You must trust me ...'

Doctor Smith is in a field hospital examining a soldier when two orderlies carry in another wounded soldier on a stretcher. They put it down on the floor. The Doctor looks at the soldier he has just been treating. 'You will be all right now, son. You can go now'. He smiles. 'Thank you, Doctor. I really appreciate your help'. He then gets up and leaves. Doctor Smith nods and then washes his hands in a metal basin on a table near the operating table. He uses the soap which is beside the dish. One of the Orderlies picks up the dish and throws the water outside the tent. He then rinses it with water from a canteen, discarding it outside again, before finally filling the dish and putting it back on the table.

Doctor Smith looks at the orderly and says, 'Thank you for that. Now, what do we have here?' The wounded soldier is now lying on the operating table. He examines the soldier's leg before looking at the orderlies. 'This leg is badly infected'. One of them looks at the doctor. 'He will probably end up losing it'. He shakes his head. 'Do not be so hasty, young man. I might just be able to save it'. The orderly looks puzzled; however, he does not say a word.

After Doctor Smith has spoken to the soldier and explained what is going to happen, one of the orderlies puts four drops of chloroform onto a rag and puts it over his mouth. He struggles. Doctor Smith looks at him and gently strokes his head. 'Calm down, son. You will be fine'.

The Doctor looks at the orderly who is helping him. 'He is out for the count now. Make sure he stays that way'. He nods without uttering a single word. The Doctor gets his instrument tray from the table behind him and puts it on the bench next to the operating table. He picks up the scalpel, makes an incision, and then cuts out some flesh before putting it into the metal dish, which is now on the tray. The orderly is intrigued. 'What are you doing?' He glances at him. 'I am cutting out the infected flesh. This will hopefully save this young man's leg'. He looks at the Doctor questioningly. 'Would it not be quicker just to take the leg off?' He stops what he is doing and shakes his head. 'It may well be quicker now, but longer term, doing it this way will be much more beneficial for this soldier'. The orderly still looks unsure. 'Most Doctors would take the leg off without giving it a second thought'. He glares at him. 'Well, I am not

'Most doctors'. He then returns to his previous
activity.

Eventually, he finishes working on the
soldier. He covers the wound with gauze,
smothered in Iodine. He then looks at the orderly.
'Change these twice daily. Then, hopefully, the
wound will heal with no infection'. He nods before
saying, 'Yes, Doctor Smith'.

Returning to the bedroom, John looks at
Doctor Smith. 'Did you save the soldier's leg? 'He
nods. 'Yes, I did. He made a full recovery and
continued to serve in the army'. He looks at the
doctor questioningly. 'So, do you think you can do
the same thing for me?' He smiles. 'I do not see
why not. I will need to go to the surgery to get my
things, though'. John nods as the Doctor continues
by saying, 'I will be back within the hour'. Without
adding to the conversation, he heads towards the
bedroom door.

Back at his surgery, Doctor Smith retrieves
his already open doctor's bag from under his desk
and places it on top it.

He then takes a key from his pocket and goes
towards the cupboard on the wall opposite the desk.
He unlocks the cupboard mentioned above and then
opens it, taking out some chloroform in a bottle,
gauze, Iodine, and his tray of surgical instruments,
which he wraps in paper, also taken from the
cupboard. He then puts the items from the

cupboard into his Doctor's bag before closing it. He then locks the cupboard door before placing the key back into his trouser pocket.

Finally, he picks the bag up from the desk before turning and heading towards the door.

As promised, within the hour, Doctor Smith, carrying his bag, enters the room with Harriet. He looks at John, who is sitting up in bed. 'Are you ready for this?' He nods. 'Yes, if this will save my leg, then you must do it. It seems like the only option, in my opinion. Doctor Smith smiles. 'Good. Let's get started then'. A couple of minutes later, the doctor hands Harriet a rag, which she gently puts over her son's face as he readies his instruments.

Four hours later, Doctor Smith smothers the stitched-up wound in Iodine as he looks at Harriet. 'Could you please burn the infected flesh that is in the tray?' Peter, who is holding a lamp, gulps before looking at his wife. 'I am pleased he got you to do that. I would be sick if he asked me'. She shakes her head at her husband, then looks at the doctor. 'Yes, of course, I can. I will wash the tray out with boiling water for you as well'. He smiles. 'Thank you. That is very much appreciated. Once I have washed up, I will get away. I will be back tomorrow and, indeed, every day to check on the patient'. She nods. 'We cannot thank you enough for what you have done, doctor'. He glances at her. 'Do not thank me yet. We still have a long way to go'. 'I know that, but at least you have given John a chance; that is all we can ask for'. He smiles. 'Indeed we have, Mrs. Wray'.

In the middle of that night, John is asleep, but he is also dreaming. It goes as follows: As he continues his charge, he is hit in the leg by a bullet. He is then hit in the arm and falls to the ground. He says to himself, 'Well, John, it looks like it is going to be up to you to get back to your trench'. Without warning, John is then shot in the head by one of the seemingly dead soldiers!

Suddenly, he wakes up with a start. He shakes his head and asks himself, 'What the hell was that?' His pillow is soaking wet with sweat. He turns it over and then tries to go back to sleep.

The following day, Doctor Smith is sitting in an easy chair in the living room. Peter and Harriet are seated at the table. He looks at them both. 'As I said last night, I will pop in every day to change the gauze and check for any infection. As long as the wound is kept clean, John should be all right'. Harriet nods. 'What can we do?' He smiles. 'If you can change the gauze at night, that would be a great help. I cannot stress enough that the wound and gauze must be kept clean at all costs. She nods once more. 'Do not worry about that; I will ensure that everything is spotless'. Peter then glances at the doctor. 'I am sorry to bring this up, but how much money do we owe you?' 'If you pay me for the gauze and Iodine, which I will keep you topped up with, that will be fine'. They both look surprised. Harriet queries further, 'What about all the time you spent operating?' He waves his arms as if to dismiss the comment. 'If I save John's leg, that will be payment enough for me'. Peter smiles and finishes the conversation by adding, 'We cannot thank you enough, Doctor. None of us will ever forget what you have done for us and, more importantly, John'. He smiles. 'It is my absolute pleasure Mr. Wray'.

Back on the road leading to Headquarters, Private Walsh glances at John. 'It sounds like Doctor Smith certainly knew what he was doing'. He nods in agreement. 'Yes, I am very fortunate that he is our family doctor. Otherwise, I probably would have had a wooden leg by now. I tell you what, though, those dreams weren't half weird the night of the operation. His compatriot gives him a questioning look. 'What do you mean?' He glances at his comrade. 'It must have been the chloroform because, as I mentioned, the dream was all mixed up'. Private Walsh nods. 'You are probably right; it could have been the chloroform. Either way, it seems very odd to have dreams like that'. He smiles. 'You are not kidding, private; they were not very nice at all; they certainly are not something that I would like to have again in a hurry'.

Chapter Ten

A little later, whilst still on their journey, Private Walsh glances at John. 'I hope you do not mind me asking you another question, but what did you do to keep yourself entertained during your recovery? I would have been bored out of my head if I were lying in bed all day, every day. His companion smiles. 'Funny that you should ask that …'

Two weeks after his operation, Harriet enters John's bedroom carrying a tray containing a bowl of stew, some bread, a spoon, and a cup containing a drink. She puts the tray on his knee, and he sits up in bed.

In between mouthfuls, John looks at his mother. 'I think I will get up today. Maybe have a walk out into town'. She shakes her head. 'Indeed, you will not, young man. Doctor Smith said you have to rest until your wound starts to knit together, and that is precisely what you will do. So, do not even think about it'. He gives her a look of frustration. 'But I am bored sitting here day after day. There are only so many newspapers and books one can read'. His mother nods. 'I know it is hard for you, son, but it is for the best. Anyway, Thomas is coming to see you later. He is bringing his chess set. Maybe you can give him a game?' He smiles. 'I had forgotten about that. It will make a pleasant change. I like Thomas'.

A few hours later, Thomas enters the bedroom carrying the chessboard and a bag in his hand. John smiles at him. 'Hello Thomas'. He returns the smile. 'Hello, lad. How are you feeling?' He glances at his father's friend. 'I am all right. Just a bit bored, to be totally honest'. He nods as he puts the chessboard and the bag on the bed before looking at him and asking, 'That is what I am here for. Are you ready for a game?' John shakes his head. 'Maybe later. Do you mind if we have a chat first?' Thomas nods. 'Yes, of course, no problem. What do you want to talk about?' He quickly looks at his chess partner. 'You were in the Zulu war, were you not?' He declares, 'Yes, I was and was very lucky to live through it'. John gives him a questioning look. How was that?' He grins. 'Do you really want to know?' He smiles. 'Yes, please. My dad has told me bits and pieces about it; I have always wanted to know more'. Thomas nods and then reveals, 'Well, if the sergeant had not sent me to get water, it could have been so different for me. Let me explain ...'

Twenty-year-old Thomas feeds the cows when the sergeant approaches him and shouts, 'O'Brien, go and fill a barrel from the water hole'. He nods. 'Yes, sergeant'. He salutes him before leaving the cow pen and heading towards the food store to pick up a barrel.

Within a few minutes, Thomas stands with the barrel outside the food store. The sergeant spots him and yells, 'Well, get going, soldier. We do not have all day. You would think you were on a day off, you lazy little sod'. He glances at him. 'Yes, Sir.' With that, he starts to roll the barrel out of the camp and towards the water hole.

Once he arrives, he starts filling the barrel. This takes a few minutes. After he is satisfied that it is full, he puts the stopper back into the top of the barrel, turns it into the rolling position, and then heads back towards the army camp. He is rolling it along the track a minute later when he hears gunfire in the distance. Without hesitating, he leaves the barrel where it is and then runs in the direction of the shooting, taking the rifle from his shoulder as he goes.

Within forty-five minutes and out of breath, Thomas arrives back at the camp, only to find that seemingly all his fellow soldiers have been killed. Amongst the dead soldiers are also the corpses of several Zulus. He checks the bodies of several of his comrades, looking for a sign of life from any of them. There is none. Suddenly, he hears a moaning coming from the direction of an upturned wagon and quickly goes to investigate.

On arrival at the site of the wagon, he finds Private Paul Jones, who is badly wounded with a spear embedded in his side, under the aforementioned wagon. Just then, a nearby wounded Zulu stirs and aims his spear at Thomas. Private Jones looks at him and shouts, 'Look out!'

Using his rifle, he quickly shoots the Zulu dead. He then drags Private Jones out from under the wagon and leans him up against it. Slowly, he starts to remove the spear from the private's side. He winces with pain and asks, 'Are you a Doctor?' He shakes his head. 'No, actually, Paul, in Civvy Street, I am not a doctor; I am a butcher, believe it or not. Some might say the professions are quite similar'. He half smiles. 'That is indeed very comforting Thomas'.

Once he has removed the spear from Private Jones' side, he covers the wound using bandages taken from a bag that happens to be close to a dead medic who is lying dead nearby. He then takes the medical bag and slings it over his other shoulder.

Later, Thomas looks around for some water bottles; he takes a couple from the bodies of his dead comrades. He also takes the pistol next to the now prone sergeant. Thomas stops and says to himself, 'This will be of more use to us than you now, sergeant'. He then heads to the food store, where he grabs some tins of meat and some biscuits before heading back to the wagon.

On his return, he puts the bottles and tins, together with the box of biscuits, into a cloth bag, which he hands to Private Jones to carry before hoisting the still heavily in pain private onto his back. Finally, he hands him the pistol before announcing, 'We have a hell of a long walk ahead of us, my friend'. Slowly, the pair vacate the camp, leaving the devastation behind them.

Once they arrive at the spot where he had left the barrel of water, Thomas carefully lays Private Jones down under a tree. The private then hands him the cloth bag. Thomas removes the bottles and fills them up. He then gives his companion a drink from one of the bottles before having one himself. Lastly, he refills the bottle before placing it into the bag and handing it back to the private. He then hoists him onto his back and says, 'Off we go again, soldier'.

The following day, Thomas is still carrying his comrade on his back. He stops walking and puts him down behind a bush. The private looks at him. 'Why have we stopped?' Thomas replies, 'I have a feeling that we are being followed'. Private Jones has a worried look on his face. 'How do you know?' 'I thought I heard running behind us. Let's wait and see. It might be nothing. That said, I do not want to be out in the open with you on my back if we are attacked. At least we have some cover here'. Private Jones nods as he checks that his pistol is loaded and then holds it at the ready. By this time, Thomas has his rifle off his shoulder and is also poised.

Two minutes later, Thomas sees four Zulus heading towards them. He takes aim and pulls the trigger. One of the quartet falls to the ground and is clearly dead. The remaining three run towards them. Whilst Thomas reloads his rifle, Private Jones takes aim with his pistol. He shoots two of them in quick succession. They drop to the ground

and are motionless. The remaining one is almost
on top of them when Thomas shoots him from
close range. He drops directly in front of them.
Private Jones looks at his companion. 'Good
shooting, my friend'. He smiles. 'You were just as
good, Private Jones'. Just then, Thomas notices one
of the other three Zulus attempting to stand up and
get to where they are with his spear poised. He
takes aim with his rifle and shoots him in the head.
Blood pours from the gaping crater that is just
being created, and he drops to the ground, and once
again, he does not move thereafter. Private Jones
smiles. 'Good shot again, Thomas'.

Shortly after, Thomas goes to check the
bodies. He finds a cloth bag next to one of them.
He opens it and pulls out some British biscuits,
together with four tins of meat. He shakes his head
before putting the food back into the bag and then
hoists it over his shoulder. He then moves the
bodies into some undergrowth and covers them up
with bushes before collecting the one near the bush
and hiding it in the same place.

On returning to the bush, Thomas looks at his
fellow private. 'I think we should stay here tonight
and hopefully get to Rorke's Drift tomorrow or the
day after at the latest. There might be some more of
them, and as I said earlier, I do not want to be
caught out in the open with you on my back'. He
nods in agreement. 'Good idea. I will take the first
watch if you want?' 'Alright. That is fine by me.
Wake me if you hear anything, anything at all'. He

takes the bag off his shoulder and puts it on the ground before looking at his companion. 'There is some more English food in there if you want some. Those Zulus must have taken it when they attacked our camp'. Paul smirks. 'It did not do them much good in the end, though. At least I do not think that we will run out now, which is a good thing'.

Two days later, inside Rorke's Drift Farmstead, a British soldier scours the landscape, looking one way and then the other. He stops, then turns around and shouts, 'There are two soldiers approaching. They look like ours. Stand by'.

An exhausted Thomas, still carrying his comrade, enters the farmstead and collapses onto the ground. Several soldiers rush to their aid. One of them asks, 'What happened?' Thomas, who can barely speak, replies quietly, 'Our camp was attacked by thousands of Zulus. I was away collecting water when I got back; everyone, apart from Private Jones, was dead. So, I decided to carry him here'. He stares at him with a look of amazement on his face. 'Let me get this right in my head. You walked almost fifty miles in this heat with a wounded man on your back?' He nods before falling unconscious through sheer exhaustion.

Back in his bedroom, John shakes his head in amazement as he looks at Thomas. 'So, you carried that soldier all the way to Rorke's Drift?' He nods.

'It is what anyone would have done in that position'. John smiles. 'I agree, but it still took guts to do that'. His father's friend shakes his head. 'Not really. Most men would do exactly the same thing'. He then quickly changes the subject by asking, 'Do you want that game of chess now?' John nods. 'Why not, my friend?'.

Returning to the trail, John glances at Private Walsh. 'Thomas came to my house three or four times a week, apart from when his wife was ill. Looking back now, he kept me sane during my recovery'. 'He certainly seems like an interesting person and also very brave from what you just told me there. Very much like you with William'. John smiles. 'To be honest, I cannot argue with that assessment with regards to Thomas. However, I did not drag William fifty miles. What he did took proper bravery. I did what anyone would do'. 'Well, I think that you are both as brave as each other, and nothing you say will ever make me think anything different'.

Chapter Eleven

Thirty minutes later, Private Walsh and John are resting. Private White is lying unconscious under a tree. John glances at him. 'I hope he is going to be alright'. He nods. 'We can only do our best for him. He has lost a lot of blood though'. 'Yes, that is my main worry'.

Shortly after, while eating some bully beef, Private Walsh looks at his companion. 'It is funny you mentioned the Zulu War earlier. My dad was involved in it but never told me about his experiences. Do you have any other stories that you can tell me, as I am really interested?' John pauses. 'Yes, but this one started when I visited Thomas' house after a Darlington match …'

John is standing watching at Feethams watching the football with Peter. Thomas joins them. He smiles at Peter, then looks at John. 'Hello, John. How have you been? Sorry, I have not been around to see you for a while, but my Olive has been ill. John glances at him. 'Yes. My dad said. Is she any better?' He nods. 'Yes, she is back to her normal self now. Thanks for asking. I was thinking, do you two fancy coming back to my house after the match for your tea?' Peter looks at his friend. 'I have to get back home straight after the game, as Harriet's friend and her husband are coming over. But John might take you up on your invitation?' John smiles. 'I would love to join you and Olive'. 'That will be great. I will see you at the main entrance after the game has finished'. He nods. Just then, there is a loud cheer from the crowd. Thomas smiles before saying, 'Well, that looks like the game is in the bag now for the lads'. John nods as his father's friend goes to rejoin Alan.

Thirty minutes after the final whistle, Thomas and John enter Thomas' living room. Olive and her neighbor Bella are both sitting sewing in easy chairs. Thomas looks at his wife and states, 'Olive, I have brought a guest home for tea. She smiles and stands up. 'It is lovely to see you again, John. You know Bella, don't you?' He nods. 'Yes, I do. Good to see you both again'. Bella smiles at him. 'Are you feeling better John?' Thomas has been keeping us up to date with your recovery'. 'I am much better now; thank you. I go back to the front next month'. She pauses for a few seconds. 'I got a letter from my son Percy the other day. He is fighting over in France'. John nods. 'I know I briefly saw him over there'. She looks surprised. 'Was he alright?' He nods. 'Yes, he seemed it. We had a brief conversation, but he had to leave. After that, I looked out for him, but unfortunately, I never saw him again'. She smiles. 'I am glad he was fit and well when you did see him; it certainly makes me feel a lot better'.

Later in the evening, Thomas, Olive, Bella and John are sitting around the table. There is a pile of plates together with some cutlery laid on top of them, pushed to one side. John looks at Olive. 'I enjoyed that meat and potato pie. It was delicious'. She smiles and then reveals, 'That is nice of you to say, but I cannot take the credit. Bella made it'. She smiles in his direction. 'I am glad you liked it'.

Shortly after, Thomas, Bella and John are still sitting at the table. The plates and cutlery have now been moved into the kitchen. John looks at his father's friend. 'Thomas, I have really enjoyed your stories about the Zulu War. Would you mind telling me another one? It would end the evening quite nicely'. Thomas looks unsure. Bella looks at John, 'I will tell you a tale about that war if you would like'. He smiles. 'I would really like that Bella'. She pauses for a few seconds and then reveals, 'It all started when ...'

Bella is polishing the living room table when her Grandfather enters the room with a letter in his hand. He looks at her with a worried look on his face. 'I have just received this letter and have found out that your Great Aunt Bella is ill. Would you mind going over to her place and checking on her for me?' She smiles, then nods. 'Not at all, Grandfather. I hope she is all right. It is not that long ago that she had that nasty fall'. He nods in agreement. 'I am sure she will be fine. I said she could come here to live with us, as we have plenty of room, but she is fiercely independent and would not hear of it'. Bella smirks. 'I wonder where she gets that from!' He plants a kiss on his Granddaughter's forehead. 'Do not be so cheeky to your elders'.

A little later, Bella starts packing food and medicines into a cloth bag. She pauses and looks at her Grandfather. 'I will take Smokey. If I cross the river, it will save me a lot of time, and I will be there long before it is dark. He looks slightly unsure. 'It is a long ride'. She nods. 'Smokey's fast. We will be there in no time'. He smiles unconvincingly. 'I know that. However, you will still need to be careful'. She stops what she is doing and smiles lovingly at her Grandfather before continuing to pack her bag. 'Honestly, I will be fine. As you know, I have made the same journey many times without any problems at all'. He half smiles. 'Yes, but that was before the Zulus were on the warpath'. 'Do not worry; as I said, I will be really careful. Anyway, I will finish getting ready; then I will set off. The quicker I get going, the quicker I will be back'.

Forty-five minutes after the conversation with her Grandfather, Bella is outside the farmstead and is ready to go. She puts her water bottle over her shoulder, along with the cloth bag. Smokey is already saddled and is tethered to the porch. Her Grandfather joins her and hands her a pistol. 'Here, take this'. She shakes her head. 'No, Grandfather, honestly, I do not need it'. He has a slightly insistent look on his face. 'Please take it, even if it is just for me. You know how worried I get about you. So, it will make me feel much better if you do what I ask'. She reluctantly takes it and puts it into the bag, along with her other belongings. She then looks at him lovingly, 'I will be back soon'. He smiles. 'Remember, be careful; I want you back here in one piece'. By this time, Bella is on the porch. She unties Smokey and then climbs onto his back. Finally, she looks at her Grandfather and returns his smile. 'I will be back before you know it'. With that, she gently digs her horse in his side with her heel, making the horse gallop out of the farmstead, leaving her concerned-looking Grandfather watching her intently until she fades from view.

Halfway through her journey, she stops near some bushes, dismounts Smokey and ties him to one of them. She then takes a drink from the bottle before pouring some of the water into a cup, which she takes from the bag, and gives her horse a drink before mopping her face with a handkerchief, once again taken from the bag. Suddenly, she hears a rustling noise and looks around, but sees nothing. She shrugs her shoulders and puts her belongings back into the bag before mounting Smokey and riding off.

A few minutes later, Bella is riding her horse when, suddenly, a spear hits the animal in the neck; it squeals and then falls to the ground. The bag falls off her shoulder and ends up under the dying horse. She is thrown from the previously mentioned horse but still manages to stand up. Unfortunately for her, before she can run to safety, two Zulus grab her and pin her to the ground.

Back at the dinner table, John looks at Bella

in amazement. 'So, how did you escape?' She smiles and reveals, 'A man named Colin saved me. Some of what I am going to reveal next is what he told me later'.

From his undercover vantage point, Colin can see a white woman (Bella) tied to a tree and four drunken Zulus pawing at her dress in an effort to get it off. One of them smiles as he fondles the woman's breasts. Eventually, they get the dress off the clearly frightened Bella. The Zulu, who was fondling her breasts, smiles as he rubs himself and stares at the now naked woman.

A fifth Zulu tries to stop what is happening by attempting to pull some of the others off Bella. One of them grabs him and holds him down, whilst another punches him several times in the face until he falls to the ground and is left unconscious. The pair laugh before turning their attention back to the helpless woman, who looks at them pleadingly and begs by shouting, 'Please stop'. The Zulus ignore her pleas and laugh even louder.

Colin is shaking and sweating. He composes himself before taking aim with his rifle.

One of the Zulus eagerly strides towards Bella, stops, and pulls off his loincloth before continuing on his goal to reach her. He then looks down at his groin area and smiles at the sight. By now, Bella is scared out of her wits and screams. In the background, his three cohorts continue to laugh.

A few seconds later, there is a loud BANG, and the naked Zulu falls to the ground with blood seeping from his head wound and is motionless. After seeing what has just happened, his three companions panic.

Colin is still shaking with fear. Eventually, he clumsily reloads the rifle. At the same time, he mutters to himself, 'Come on, Colin. Get your damned arse into gear'. He then takes aim again and hits another of the captors in the leg. The unfortunate Zulu drops to the ground in pain as Bella struggles to free herself. After several attempts, she manages to get loose, quickly puts her dress back on and then launches herself at the injured man, who is by now gingerly standing up. She knocks him back to the ground with a single hard punch. Due to the force of it, his head hits a tree, and after that, he does not move.

Meanwhile, Colin aims his rifle at the remaining kidnappers. There is another loud BANG, and one of the surviving two is hit in the head and drops to the ground, and is obviously dead. The other one races towards the direction of the shot as Colin aims his rifle and fires again. His opponent is once again hit in the head. He falls to the ground and does not move thereafter.

By this time, the injured Zulu is trying to get up. Blood is seeping from his deep head wound. Bella grabs an empty bottle and hits him over the head several times with it. As a result, he ends up

on the ground and, like most of his friends, is now
dead.

Bella sees Colin enter the camp and hurriedly
retreats, still brandishing the now broken,
bloodstained bottle. She is shaking, and tears are
streaming heavily down her face.

Colin shoulders his gun, puts his hands up
before heading towards her. 'Hey, whoa, you are all
right now.' She half-smiles. 'I think I am'. Colin
nods, then heads towards her. 'I'm not going to hurt
you'. She retreats and screams, 'Get away, stay
away from me'. She takes a further step back and
then cowers. He removes the gun from his shoulder
before putting it onto the ground, ensuring that it is
within easy reach. He then places his jacket around
the woman's shoulders before offering her a drink
of water from his canteen and suggests, 'Here, this
might help'. She takes the canteen, then half smiles
at Colin and says, 'Thanks'. She takes a drink,
replaces the top on the canteen and then hands it
back to him. He sits near the woman, at her level
and looks at her. 'I am Colin'. She nods and then
quietly replies, 'Bella'. He looks at her. 'Are you
hurt?' She shakes her head. 'No. I am fine, just
shaken up. I will tell you what; I have never been
so frightened in my life'. He nods understandingly.
'Do not worry, you are safe now'.

Shortly after, she removes Colin's jacket from
her shoulders and hands it back to him. Just then,
the Zulu who tried to help her begins to stir. Colin

notices and rushes towards him. Bella glares at him and shouts, 'No! Do not hurt him'. He stops. She then walks over to him and helps him up. He stares at Colin but does nothing. She looks at him, smiles and then says, 'Uya manje. Siyabonga ngokuzama ungisindise'. He nods at her and then leaves the camp without taking his eyes off Colin, who then looks at Bella. 'What did you say to him?' She replies, 'I told him to go and thanked him for trying to save me'. He looks surprised. 'Should we not have killed him? He might go and get help and then come after us'. She shakes her head. 'No, I honestly do not think he will do that simply because I could tell that he was a good man'. He looks unsure but nods in partial agreement. 'Fair enough. You know these people better than I do'.

Back at Thomas' dinner table, John looks at Bella. That was amazing. I am sorry that happened to you, it must have been really frightening, but I have one question'. 'What is that?' 'I meant to ask Thomas before when he has mentioned him in conversation, but what happened to Colin?' She looks at Thomas, then John. 'He was killed later in the war'. He shakes his head. 'That is a real shame. He sounded like a very brave man'. She smiles. 'He was John, very much so'.

Ten minutes later, John gets up from his seat. He looks at Thomas and Bella. 'I have had a really nice time. Your stories about the Zulu War have inspired me for whatever lies ahead. I want to thank you both for that'. He gets up and offers his hand to his friend's son. He shakes it before continuing, 'I have to be going. Thanks again for a lovely evening'. Thomas smiles. 'It has been great having you here, lad. I will see you again before you leave for the front, no doubt'. He nods. 'Yes, you will. I am determined to beat you at chess at least once before I go'. He laughs at the comment and jokingly states, 'We will see'. Bella stands up and gives John a peck on the cheek. 'I have enjoyed the evening too; I hope everything goes all right for you when you head back to the front'. 'I am sure they will, Bella. I hope Percy gets through it unscathed as well'. She smiles. 'Me too, he is my life'. He nods. 'Anyway, I will bid you both good night'. After a few seconds, he sets off, leaving a smiling Thomas and Bella behind him.

Back to the present, Private Walsh glances at his companion. 'That Bella was lucky that Colin was there at the right time to save her. The story reminded me of that woman in the farmhouse earlier today'. 'Yes, she sprang to mind as I told you the tale. I hope she managed to get those Germans buried without any problems'. His compatriot nods. 'I hope so too, but there is nothing that we can do about that now, my friend'.

Chapter Twelve

Later in their journey, John stops walking, looks across the fields, then turns and glances at Private Walsh, who is now carrying Private White. 'I think I can see a building in the distance. All being well, Private White should be able to rest there. Come on, let's go and take a look. His comrade stops walking and looks in the direction John had just a few seconds earlier. 'Yes, I can definitely see something. Come on, let's go and have a look'. They slowly start walking again and head towards the building.

Shortly after, the pair can clearly see a barn and head towards it.

A couple of minutes later, they approach the stone building and quickly notice that the door is open.

The two men slowly enter; John has his rifle poised.

They quickly look around and soon see the body of a dead British soldier who still has his rifle by his side. As they look up, they hear rustling noises coming from the barn loft above. Private Walsh carefully puts the now semi-conscious

Private White down. He then removes his rifle from his shoulder.

In the barn loft, Hans is crouched, looking down.

John glances at his companion. 'You stay here with Private White. I will go and see who or what is in the loft'. He readies his rifle and looks at John. 'Be careful'. He nods and then slowly walks across the barn to the ladder and starts climbing up it.

Hans is poised and ready to attack before recognizing him. Very quietly, he says, 'John! It is me, Hans'. He hears the familiar voice and stops climbing. 'Hans. Is that you?' From the barn loft, the German reveals, 'Yes, it is. Come up'.

Once he is in the barn loft, John glances at his friend. After a few seconds, he smiles at him briefly, then his expression changes to one of seriousness. 'Hans, there are two other British soldiers in the barn. One is badly wounded'. He has a concerned expression as his friend looks at him. 'Do not worry; it will be fine. We will have to think of something'.

Chapter Thirteen

As he looks around the loft, John is shocked to see two British soldiers tied up in the corner of the loft. Hans now has a pistol pointed at them. He glances at his friend. 'I had to do it. They were going to kill me'. Just then, Private Walsh shouts from below, 'Is everything all right up there?' John pauses and then shouts back, 'Yes, everything is fine. Give me a minute, and then come up'. The private shouts back, 'No problem'. A confused looking John glances at Hans. 'I honestly do not know what to do about you being here'.

A few minutes later, Private Walsh appears in the loft and is taken aback when he sees Hans pointing his pistol at the two British soldiers. He glares at Hans and then John. 'What the hell is going on here?' He looks at his comrade. 'This is Hans, my friend from Cambridge University, the one I told you about. He said that he had no choice other than to kill the soldier in the barn and take the other two captive'. He continues to glare at John. 'We need to set them free and take your friend prisoner. It is the proper thing to do'. John glances at Private Walsh. 'Before we decide what to do, let me explain our friendship. His companion looks unsure but nods gingerly.

The year is 1909, and Christmas decorations adorn the Wray family living room. A Christmas tree is also in the corner as John, his parents, and

Hans tuck into their Christmas dinners.

Later in the afternoon, the table is cleared as Peter looks at John and Hans. 'It is time to open our gifts, boys'. John hands his father a present. A minute later, his friend does likewise. Firstly, Peter opens the gift from John. A blue tie is revealed. He smiles and then rips open Hans' package. It's another tie; this time, it's brown. He continues to smile. 'At least I will not run out of ties, boys. Joking apart, these are great. Every time I ever wear one of them for work, I will be reminded of today'. Hans also smiles. 'That is a lovely thing to say, Mr. Wray'.

Meanwhile, Harriet does not participate in the proceedings. Hans is puzzled by this and looks at her. 'If you do not mind me asking, why do you not take part in Christmas with the rest of your family?' She smiles at the young German. 'I am Jewish, so we do not celebrate it'. He gives her a knowing look as John turns to his friend. 'When I was old enough, I chose to follow Christianity like my father; however, we both still fully respect the Jewish faith'. He looks at John's parents. 'It was good that John was given the choice. I respect all faiths. That is how I was brought up, especially by my father'. She smiles. 'That is a good thing to hear, Hans. Unfortunately, not everyone is like you and your father'. Peter smiles and then looks at the pair. 'Changing the subject for a moment, do you two fancy coming to the football tomorrow? My beloved Darlington are playing at home'. Hans looks at him. 'I would love to go, Peter'. John smirks. 'I very much doubt that you will be saying that after you have seen them play'. Peter grins at his son. 'Very funny, John, we will get into the Football League one day; mark my words. He smiles at his father. 'With supporters like you, dad, I am sure they will'. Peter smiles, then looks at the pair. 'Anyway, enough about football for today. You two need to open your presents'. Both men smile as they pick up their gifts.

The following day, John, Hans and Peter are at Feethams, watching the game against Spennymoor. Thomas, who has just entered the ground, spots the trio and quickly heads towards them.

A minute later, Peter gestures towards Hans, then looks at his friend. 'Thomas, this is Hans, John's friend from Cambridge University'. He smiles, and then shakes his hand. 'Good to meet you, lad. Are you enjoying the match?' He nods. 'Yeah, very much so. I have never been to a game before; it is all very exciting'. He glances at the German whilst watching the match. 'Hopefully, it will not be your last son, but remember not every game will be as good as this one'. 'I understand, Sir, and if I ever return to England, I will certainly come back again'. Hans replies. Thomas nods in his direction, then turns to Peter. 'Alec Fraser is having a good game today. He took his goal really well'. John smiles. 'Thomas, is that not the lad from Inverness?' His father is taken aback by the observation and looks at his son with a surprised expression on his face. 'How in the world did you know that?' He smiles. 'I read the newspapers, dad, as I like to keep up with your football team, as and when I can'. He smirks. 'I think you are a closet Darlington supporter really'. He shakes his head. 'I would not quite go that far, but I have to admit, I do take a little bit of an interest. After all, they are my home town club'. Thomas smiles and looks at the trio. 'Well, lads, I am going to stand with Alan; he will think I have got lost. If I do not see you later, I hope you all enjoy the rest of your Christmas.' Peter nods. 'The same to you, Thomas; hopefully, we will catch up after the match'.

After the game, John, Hans and Peter are leaving the ground as Thomas joins them and excitedly says, 'That was a good result today, lads, 2-0 against Spennymoor, especially as they look like winning the league this season'. Peter nods in agreement. 'Yes, I would have taken that before kick-off'. He quickly glances at his friend. 'I cannot argue about that, to be honest. Anyway, I have to dash; the wife does not like me being late for my tea. Oh, by the way, I nearly forgot, when are you back managing that bank of yours? We could have a drink before you return to the grind'. 'Good idea. I am back at my desk on 2nd January. I was owed some holidays, so I took them whilst John and Hans were here. But I will meet you tomorrow night for a couple of pints if you want?' Thomas smiles at his friend. 'Yes, that would be great. Is around seven in The Coachman all right?' Peter nods. 'I will see you then. I might bring Harriet, but could you bring Olive if you'd like? We could make it a foursome'. 'I think she would like that. Anyway, I must go. As I said, she hates me getting home late for my tea'. He then looks at John and Hans before continuing. 'Good seeing you, John. Hans, I hope to see you again sometime'. Before they can answer, he has sprinted off down the street ahead of them. Peter laughs. 'He has always been like that ever since we were at school together. It is quite amusing, to be honest'.

A year later, John looks at Hans as they stroll through the Keiser Wilhelm Park. He briefly touches Hans' hand. 'This is a beautiful place. You are very lucky to live so close to it'. The German smiles. 'Yes, it is and indeed I am. I actually came to the park's opening back in 1906 with my parents. It was actually designed by Walter Von Engelhardt. Interestingly, according to local records, which I have checked, part of the area that is now the park was a slaughterhouse in the late 1870s'. John shakes his head. 'You certainly know your local history, Hans'. He nods. 'Of course I do. It is something I have always been interested in. That is why I chose it as my degree subject at Cambridge'. The German then glances at his friend before continuing, 'Come on. We had better get back. My parents are going out tonight'. He nods. 'No problem at all'.

Shortly after, John is sitting at the table with Hans and his parents, Hans Senior and Gertrude.

Four empty plates and four sets of cutlery are neatly stacked in the corner of the table.

Hans Senior looks at John. 'So, have you enjoyed your stay here in Dusseldorf?' He smiles. 'Yes, very much so, Hans. I am really grateful to you both for letting me stay here'. Hans Senior waves his hands dismissively. 'No problem at all. You are welcome here anytime'. 'Thank you for that; I am extremely grateful'. He nods, gets up from the table and looks at his wife. 'Come on, Gertrude. We had better get changed. Your sister will be expecting us for our weekly card game soon'. She gets up from the table but does not utter a single word.

Back in the barn loft, Private Walsh shakes his head. 'So, what, you two became good friends. That is not enough. I still think we need to do the

right thing. We have to, as we owe it to our country
and, more importantly, in my opinion, to ourselves'.

Chapter Fourteen

Back in his quarters, the officer checks his watch and says to himself, 'Those three are taking a long time. I wonder what is keeping them'. He then gets up and heads towards the trench.

Five minutes later, he approaches the sergeant. 'Privates Wray, Walsh and White are not back yet. I really do need to get that letter through to headquarters. We will give them until the morning; if they have not returned, we will send three more men to achieve the objective'. The sergeant glances at him. 'Private Wray is an excellent soldier; if anyone can accomplish the job, it will be him'. 'How come you know him so well?' The sergeant smiles as he thinks back. 'I have fought with him before in Flanders. Let me explain...'

John and his comrades wait in their trench as they are bombarded by German artillery. He looks at the sergeant, who is next to him. 'The officer told me a few minutes ago that most of the German trenches have been hit, and many of their soldiers have been killed'. He smiles nervously. 'That may be true, lad, but I bet there are still plenty of them left once we get over there'.

Ten minutes later, the officer blows his whistle and leads John and his comrades over the top. They make it to the wire, but many of them are hit by the German machine guns. John says quietly to himself, 'It looks like the officer was wrong about their trenches being destroyed. We were told that it would be a walk in the park. Some walk in the park, this has turned out to be'. The sergeant, who is running alongside John, hears his thoughts but says nothing.

Shortly after, the officer is hit. John stops to check on him, but he is dead. his left arm is missing, and blood is coming out of both his mouth and nose. He shakes his head, then quickly retrieves his pistol and puts it into his own belt. He then leads the charge and is followed by the sergeant, who is slowed down by a flesh wound to his leg. However, he still continues his journey towards the German trench.

Shortly after, John and his remaining comrades climb into the aforementioned German trench and quickly set out, making the area safe and rounding up several German prisoners in the process.

He continues to search the trench when suddenly, a German soldier comes at him with his bayonet. He dodges it by stepping to one side, then quickly retrieves the officer's pistol from his belt and shoots the soldier, who falls to the ground. The German is not dead. He is about to help him when a British comrade runs from behind him and finishes him off with his bayonet. John looks at him and shouts, 'There was no need for that. He was helpless. That is not what war is all about'. The soldier sniggers, 'Helpless or not, in my opinion, the only good German is a dead German and one final thing, I fight my own war, not any other officers or soldiers'. John shakes his head in disgust as the British soldier walks away, laughing to himself. Unseen by either John or the soldier, the now badly limping sergeant has stopped walking, is leaning against some sandbags, and has witnessed everything that has just happened. Like his comrade, he shakes his head in disbelief.

Later in Neuve Chapelle, the inhabitants welcome John and his comrades after they have taken the village. They round up the captured Germans and put them under guard in the village square. The wounded sergeant is laid on a stretcher, waiting to be treated, and once again, he watches the proceedings with great interest. A British soldier looks at the German captives and smirks in their direction. He then shouts, 'Let's shoot them all'. John steps in and shouts in his direction, 'Whilst I am here, no one harms the prisoners'. 'Who the hell put you in charge?' He stays calm and collected. 'No one, but you will have to shoot me first'. The soldier shrugs his shoulders, then starts to walk away and shouts, 'Have it your own way, but it would be easier to shoot them, in my opinion'.

Once again, while waiting for his leg to be treated, the sergeant witnesses what has just happened and how John had dealt with it.

Back in the British trench, the officer glances at the sergeant. 'It sounds like Private Wray has excellent leadership qualities'. He nods. 'He went to Cambridge University and could have joined the army as an officer, but he turned the opportunity down and enlisted as a private'. The officer shrugs his shoulders. 'He must have had his reasons for coming to that decision, sergeant'. His subordinate adds, 'I suppose you are right, Sir; it just seems such a waste of talent to me; that is all'. 'I cannot disagree with you there'.

Chapter Fifteen

Meanwhile, back in the barn loft, an anxious Private Walsh looks at John. 'We are at war with Germany. We have to do the right thing. We have no choice'. He nods in partial agreement. 'I know, but we could let Hans go; no one would be any the wiser and then we can all walk away from this'. The private shakes his head. 'Too many people know. We could both end up in front of a firing squad if this ever got out. I am certainly not prepared to risk that happening to me'.

Whilst this conversation is going on, a very nervous-looking Hans still has his pistol firmly pointed at the hostages.

Chapter Sixteen

The following morning, back in the British trench, the officer heads towards the sergeant and shouts, 'Sergeant, Private Wray and the other lads still are not back, so take two men and try and find out what has happened to them'. He salutes the officer. 'Yes, Sir'. The officer takes a letter out of his trouser pocket, hands it to his subordinate and states, 'If you do not find them, make sure that at least one of you gets this letter through to headquarters. It is vitally important; therefore, this must be your priority. If you don't find them quickly, it might be a good idea to split up, but I'll leave that decision up to you. He folds the letter and puts it into his top pocket. 'Yes, Sir'.

Five minutes later, the sergeant looks at two soldiers who are finishing their bread and jam and orders in a loud voice, 'Privates Wright and Carter, get your stuff ready; you two lucky gentlemen are coming on a little outing with me. Be ready in ten minutes'. Private Carter looks at the sergeant questioningly. 'Where are we going, Sir?' He replies, 'You will find out soon enough, private. Now get your backsides into gear'.

Once the sergeant is out of hearing distance, Private Carter glances at his comrade. 'I wonder where we are going? Private Wright smiles. 'As the sergeant said, we will find out soon enough. At least we will be out of this stinking trench for a while'. His companion nods. 'Yes, I was thinking about it in exactly the same way'. Come on, let's get our stuff ready'.

About three hours later, two miles away, the German trench is under heavy bombardment from the British artillery. Sergeant Muller goes over to two of his comrades (Privates Werner and Braun), who are crouched down trying to avoid the falling shells. 'You two, the Commandant wants you two to try and find Private Eckhart. He was supposed to be back with vital information by now, but has not returned'. Private Werner salutes the sergeant. 'Yes, Sir'.

Without saying another word, the two privates begin to gather their belongings.

Chapter Seventeen

Back at the barn loft, the conversation has continued all night. A weary-looking John looks at Private Walsh. 'There must be another way out of this that suits us all'. He shakes his head. 'I honestly cannot see any other option apart from what I have already said'.

Just then, there is a noise coming from the barn, and Private White can be heard shouting, 'What is happening up there?' John glances at his fellow private. 'You go down and make sure that he is alright'. He looks unsure and starts to explain by saying, 'But …' John glares at him and cuts him off mid-sentence by shouting, 'I am still in charge, private. Now do as you are told soldier'. Without uttering another word, a furious Private Walsh heads towards the ladder.

Hans (who still has his pistol pointed at the hostages) glances at John. 'What are we going to do?' He spreads his hands in a gesture of not knowing. 'I need time to think, Hans'.

Just then, Private Walsh shouts from the barn, 'I will be a few minutes. Private White is not looking good at all. He has lost a lot of blood. I will re-bandage his leg because the one he has on is soaked through. John, you need to make up your mind about what you want to do because we cannot go on like this'. John looks at the German with a worried look on his face, but does not say a word.

Chapter Eighteen

Around the same time, the sergeant and Privates Carter and Wright are running towards headquarters. Private Wright looks at the sergeant. 'I wonder what happened to Private Wray and the other two?' He glances at his companion. 'I have no idea, private. But I guess we will find out soon enough'.

Shortly after, Private Carter looks at the sergeant. 'You know, I hope that we find John; I feel like I owe him one because he saved my life a few years back. He does not look surprised at all. 'What happened?' The private grimaces at the memory before continuing, 'Well, it all started when …

Private Carter, dressed in a British soldier's uniform, is being chased by another man who is carrying a knife. By sheer coincidence, John is heading in the same direction as the two men had done a few seconds earlier.

In what seems like no time at all, he finds Private Carter leaning against a shop door with blood flowing from his stomach. He looks very concerned. 'That does not look too good to me at all. I live two minutes' walk from here. I will take you to my house, and then I will get you some help'. Private Carter smiles weakly. 'Thanks, mate. I really appreciate this'.

Within five minutes, John is hammering on his front door. Peter initially has a stern look on his face and starts to ask, 'Why haven't you got your?' ... He then sees the soldier's wound and, for a few seconds, seems unsure what to do and simply stands there. John glares at him and shouts, 'Dad. Can you give me a hand, please?' His father emerges from his momentary trance. 'Of course I can, son. I am sorry'. He then grabs one of the soldiers' arms and helps him to get the injured man into their house.

Once in the living room, John and Peter sit the soldier down in an easy chair. Peter shouts to his wife, who is in the kitchen. 'Harriet, have we got any bandages? We have a young man here who has been stabbed'. She shouts back, 'Oh my God! I will be right there'.

Harriet arrives in the living room shortly after. She has a tin in her hand, which she opens and takes out a bandage. Meanwhile, Peter looks at the soldier. 'What is your name, son?' 'Benjamin. Private Benjamin Carter'. Harriet, by now, has Benjamin's uniform top lifted up and is wrapping the bandage around the wound. After she is finished, she looks at the soldier. 'I think you need to see a Doctor. Just to be on the safe side, because your cut is very deep'. John glances at his mother. 'Do you think that I should go and get Doctor Smith?' She smiles and then nods. 'I think you had better do just that, son'. With that, he rushes out of the room without saying another word.

Twenty minutes later, he arrives back in the living room with Doctor Smith, who immediately goes over to Private Carter. He removes the bandage that Harriet had applied and then examines the wound. 'I will stitch this up for you. It could have been a lot worse, young man. Another inch and the knife would have pierced your heart, and you would have been dead instantly'. The private nods in the Doctor's direction. 'It is certainly a relief that it didn't do that. Thank you for coming and sorting me out so quickly. I will pay you after I have been home. I was robbed by the man who stabbed me'. 'That is no problem at all. It is what I am here for. Now, lie back'. Benjamin does as he is asked, and then the Doctor stitches up the wound.

Once Doctor Smith has finished packing his bag, Peter looks at him. 'How much does Benjamin owe you Doctor?' He stops what he is doing. 'Tuppence'. He fishes into his trouser pocket, takes out some coins, and then gives him the money he is owed. He takes it and puts it into his own pocket. 'Thank you very much, but it could have waited. Anyway, I have to go. I have a young lady who is almost due to give birth at any time,

and I need to check in on her. Harriet glances at
the Doctor. 'I will see you out'. Benjamin looks at
Doctor Smith. 'Thanks for your help'. He nods in
his direction. 'No problem at all, young man. If you
need those stitches taken out in a few weeks' time,
I live at number four Alfred Street; I will be able to
do it for you'. He nods. 'I will do that, Doctor.
Thanks again'. He smiles and then follows Harriet
out of the room.

Once the Doctor has left, Benjamin glances at
Peter. 'Thanks for paying that for me. It was very
much appreciated. I will pay you back. I promise'.
John's father shakes his head. 'Do not worry about
it, son. It is the least that I can do'. The private
smiles. 'That is very kind of you Sir'.

A few minutes later, Peter looks at his guest.
'Are you going to get the police to investigate the
attack on you?' He nods. 'Yes, of course I am. I
will go to the Police Station later today or
tomorrow at the latest.' Peter smiles. 'I think that
you are doing the right thing. Try to go today if you
can, though'.

Shortly after, Benjamin gets up to leave.
Harriet, who is now back in the living room, looks
at him. 'Would you like John to walk home with
you?' He nods. 'Yes, please. That would be great. I
do not feel very well at all and will probably go to
bed when I get home'. She looks concerned. 'Is
there anyone there to look after you once you get

back to your house?' He nods. 'Yes, I live with my mother. I will get her to go to the police station with me once I feel better'.

Later, on their way to Private Carter's house, John looks at his newly found friend. 'So, what made you join the army?' He pauses. 'I just wanted to see the world. To be fair, it turned out to be the best thing I ever did'. He glances at Benjamin. 'I am just a Trainee Journalist'. Benjamin smiles. 'There is nothing wrong with that, mate, but if you want to broaden your horizons, the army is certainly the place to do it'. John is clearly impressed by what he has just heard. 'It is definitely worth thinking about. I have always fancied, as you said, 'broadening my horizons'.

Returning to the present, the sergeant glances at Private Carter. 'I always thought there was something special about that lad'. He then pauses and continues. 'As a matter of interest, when did this happen?' The private states, 'About nine months before the war started'. He looks at the sergeant and then adds, 'Even though we both live in Darlington, I never saw him again during those nine months until he returned to the front after he was wounded. Thinking about it now, it is a little strange'. He smiles at the comment. 'Sometimes these things can happen in life, private'.

Shortly after, Private Wright looks at the pair. 'Didn't Private Wray also drag someone back to our trench from no man's land despite being badly wounded himself?' The sergeant looks shocked on hearing what has just been said. 'I did not know anything about that. I must have been in a different platoon at the time'. Private Wright continues. 'When he was fit to return to the front, he asked to be moved to another platoon as he did not want people to know. I only found out because I know William's brother'. The sergeant glances at the private. 'Who is William?' He smiles. 'He is the soldier that Private Wray dragged to safety'. The sergeant looks at both of his men. 'I honestly did not know anything about this'. 'Neither does anyone else apparently'. The sergeant pauses to think for a few seconds and then issues the following order, 'You two, keep this to yourselves. It is best to respect Private Wray's wishes, as he obviously wants to try to keep this to himself'. Both men nod and then say in unison, 'Yes, sergeant'.

Chapter Nineteen

Meanwhile, John looks down the ladder towards the barn and shouts, 'Private Walsh, what is happening with Private White?' From the barn, He shouts back, 'I am struggling to stop the bleeding. He lost a lot of blood when we were carrying him here. He is out of it again'. 'Is he going to be alright?' John shouts. Private Walsh sighs. 'To be honest, I think he is too far gone. He needs more help than I can give him. I am not a trained medic'. He looks concerned and shouts back, 'Try your best'. The private shouts, 'That is exactly what I am doing, John'.

Hans glances at his friend and states, 'We need to decide what we are going to do'. He nods nervously before responding, 'I know, Hans. I know'.

At precisely the same time, Private Werner and his companion are marching in the direction of the barn. Private Werner glances at his comrade. 'I wonder why finding Private Eckhart is so important?' 'He is supposed to be really good at collecting intelligence. That is probably the reason'. He nods in agreement. 'Yeah, that makes sense. Do you know him?' Private Braun pauses. 'I do. We are both from Dusseldorf, and we went to the same school. But we were not very close at all'. Private Werner nods. 'I have spoken to him a few times. From what he has said, he clearly enjoys his history. He went to Cambridge University in England to study it'. Private Werner smirks. 'Do you think he is a little bit odd?' His companion looks puzzled. 'What do you mean?' Private Werner retorts, 'He is very studious, not really the army type, in my opinion'. Private Braun shakes his head. 'There is nothing wrong with that. He is cleverer than a lot of the guys. To be honest, I think some of them are envious of him'. His compatriot nods in agreement. 'I think you could be right. It is not his fault in the slightest that he is different'.

Back in the barn loft, Hans still has his pistol aimed at the two hostages. Private Walsh once again shouts up from the barn, 'I think I am losing him. He is bleeding everywhere!' John looks down towards the barn and shouts, 'You need to apply direct pressure on the bandage'. A now extremely flustered Private Walsh shouts, 'I have done that. But I lifted it to check whether the bleeding had stopped. It is running like a waterfall now'. John shakes his head and yells, 'You should not have done that'. 'Shit! I know that now!' he exclaims.

Chapter Twenty

Almost simultaneously, the sergeant and Privates Carter and Wright are marching towards headquarters. Private Carter looks down the road and then glances at the sergeant. 'What is that sticking out of the ditch in the distance?' He struggles to see. 'I think it looks like a body'. He then looks at Private Wright and continues. 'Go and check it out. Private Carter and I will cover you'. The private checks that his rifle is loaded, then glances at his commanding officer. 'Yes, Sir'. He then slowly sets off towards where they think the body is.

The sergeant and Private Carter crouch down at the side of the road with their rifles at the ready.

Back in the barn, Private Walsh is still struggling to stem the blood flow coming from Private White's leg. He continues to press the bandage hard on the wound. His fellow private is now conscious. He looks pleadingly at his comrade. 'Please do not let me die. I have not seen my baby son yet, and it is my dream to do so'. Private Walsh briefly touches his hand and smiles. 'So, you live in York? I found the story you told us of how you got there really interesting. As you said earlier, your parents certainly made the correct decision to move there. His companion responds weakly. 'Yes, York is a great place to live. That is for sure'. Private Walsh looks at the now even weaker Private White. 'I agree; I have been there before. It is a beautiful city, as you said. And do not worry, you will see your wife again, and you will also meet your little lad'. Private White shakes his head, then glances at his companion. 'I do not think so, my friend. If you are honest, you will know that. Private Walsh does not utter a word as his stricken friend continues. 'Can you look in my top pocket? There are two letters in there; one for my parents and the other for my wife. If you get out of here alive, will you please make sure that they get them?' He nods, then puts the letters into his own pocket. 'Of course I will; you have my word'. His comrade then starts to drift off. The look on Private Walsh's face turns to one of worry. He pauses for a few seconds, then checks for a heartbeat coming from his colleague. He quickly realizes that there is not one. He pauses for a few seconds, shakes his head and then closes his companion's eyes for the very last time. After a few seconds, he heads towards the barn loft ladder.

Chapter Twenty-One

Meanwhile, Privates Werner and Braun continue their journey. Private Braun glances at his comrade. 'How do we know that Private Eckhart came this way?' He smiles. 'Because Sergeant Muller told me he did. Apparently, he was sent to gather information on British troop numbers and such like'. Private Braun gestures in a questioning way, using his arms. 'He could have got into a fight with British soldiers and be dead for all we know'. His fellow German pauses for a few seconds. 'That is what we need to find out. I get the feeling that you do not like him very much'. Private Braun shakes his head. 'It is not that at all'. He looks at his companion. 'Well, what is your problem then?' Private Braun thinks for a few seconds, then glances at his fellow German. 'I simply do not think it is worth the risk of sending us two out to find him. That is my honest opinion'. 'That is a fair point. But who are we to argue with our Commanders? They must have their reasons'. 'I suppose you are right. Let's hope we find him soon, dead or alive', his compatriot says, a comment which abruptly ends the conversation.

Around the same time, a visibly upset Private Walsh enters the barn loft. He looks at John. 'I tried my best John, but Private White has passed away. I stayed with him until the end. He was telling me about his baby son, whom he has not seen. It was all very sad'. He then hands him the two letters. 'He gave me these to post. Given that you are in charge, I think you should have them'. John puts the letters into his pocket and then glances at his comrade. 'I know you will have done your best to save him. As you said, it is all very sad. Private Walsh nods, then looks at the hostages, Hans and finally John. 'I need some air. I am going outside. When I get back, we need to decide on our next course of action; as I said earlier, we simply cannot go on like this'. He then heads towards the ladder without uttering another word. Both John and Hans have worried looks on their faces as the private leaves the loft.

Chapter Twenty-Two

At around the same time, Private Wright comes across the two dead German soldiers. He looks around and sees that there is no one else in the vicinity. He turns carefully around and then walks back in the direction he came.

Less than five minutes later, he is back with his fellow soldiers. He glances at the sergeant. 'Sir, there are two dead Germans in a ditch just up the road. I could not see you properly to signal you, so I returned to let you know. He nods in the direction of the private. He then looks at both of his subordinates. 'Come on, you two. I want to take a look at these bodies for myself. There might be some clues as to the possible whereabouts of our men, you never know'. The trio slowly head towards the ditch with their rifles poised.

Shortly after, the sergeant is in the ditch looking at the two dead German soldiers. He glances at a patch of ground a little way from the bodies and notices a pool of blood. As he looks a little further, he notices a trail of blood leading away from the ditch and into the countryside. He smiles at the other two soldiers. 'It could be that I have just found where our lads have gone'. Private Carter glances at him. 'How do we know it is definitely them Sir?' He looks at the private. 'We do not know for sure. However, we will soon find out. Come on, lads, let's get moving. He then climbs out of the ditch, and the threesome start to follow the trail of blood.

In the meantime, Privates Werner and Braun are still heading in the direction of the barn. 'Private Werner glances at his colleague. 'I think we should take a detour; we have been on this road for quite a few miles. Maybe we should go across country'. 'That is fine by me, my friend'.

The duo head off the road and go towards a field. Private Werner glances at his comrade. 'This could actually save us some time'. Private Braun smirks. 'I certainly hope so. I am getting sick of looking for Eckhart now. I would much prefer to be back in our trench behind my machine gun, killing British soldiers rather than messing about around here, going around in never-ending circles'.

Chapter Twenty-Three

Private Walsh is now back in the barn loft.
Hans, who still has the pistol pointed at the
hostages, looks at him. 'As has already been said, if
you let me go, no one ever needs to know what
happened'. He glances at the two hostages. 'What
about those two?' Hans smiles, and then, without
warning, he shoots them both. They keel over and
are obviously dead. After a few seconds, He half
smiles and then states, 'Problem solved. They
cannot tell anyone now because they are dead'.
Private Walsh is clearly shocked by what has just
happened and tries to get his rifle from his
shoulder. John quickly grabs the pistol from Hans,
points it at the private, and then advises, 'I would
not do that if I were you'. He puts his hands up and
angrily shouts, 'I cannot believe you have sided
with a German. You are a traitor'. He pauses. 'I
have my reasons, private'. He shakes his head in
disbelief. 'I would love to know what they are. Call
yourself a British soldier; you are a disgrace to the
uniform'. John remains calm as he ends the
conversation. 'All will be revealed in good time as
to why I am doing this, trust me'.

Meanwhile, as they walk through the
countryside, Private Werner stops and looks at the
ground. He notices two blood trails and glances at
his comrade. 'What do you make of these?' He

pauses, then looks at the trails. 'I think that we need to follow one trail or the other'. Private Werner nods in agreement. 'I think you are right. Come on. We will follow the one on the left'. The pair set off following their chosen trail.

At precisely the same time, the sergeant glances at the two privates. 'We will stop here for a ten-minute break, have something to eat and then get going again'. Privates Carter and Wright stop marching and sit down on the grass. The sergeant sits down next to them. Private Carter glances at him. 'Hopefully, we will find our lads soon. I am due a couple of rest days away from the trench in three days, and I do not want to miss those'. He smiles as he opens a tin of Bully Beef. 'I think we will be back long before then, lad. So, I would not worry about it if I were you'.

In the meantime, Privates Braun and Werner arrive at the ditch. They quickly notice the two dead German soldiers. Private Werner climbs in. He quickly checks the two bodies by feeling their skin. He then glances at his companion. 'They are both stone cold. That tells me that they have been dead for quite a few hours'. He then checks the pockets of the dead soldiers, takes out their IDs, and puts them into his own pocket. He also looks around the ditch and glances at his fellow private. 'There is a pool of blood here. Leading away from it, there is a trail, which I think we should follow. It could lead us to Private Eckhart'. Private Braun climbs into the ditch. He looks at the blood trail and then gives Private Werner a questioning look. 'It might not, though. There is no evidence at all that Private Eckhart has been here'. His fellow traveler nods. 'You could be right. At least if we look and do not find anything, we can go back to our lines and honestly tell Sergeant Muller that we did our best and found nothing'. 'As usual, I suppose you are right. Come on, let's go. The sooner we get this over with, the better, in my opinion'.

The pair climb out of the ditch and follow the trail of blood at a breakneck pace.

Two minutes later, the sergeant looks at his companions. 'Pack up, lads. We need to get moving'. The two privates put their belongings away and follow the sergeant who is already on his way. Private Wright looks at his comrade and smirks. 'He is keen'. Private Carter returns the smirk and then nods. 'He certainly is my friend. He is a man on a mission'. His colleague laughs loudly. 'We all are'.

Chapter Twenty-Four

Back in the barn loft, Private Walsh is now sitting down. He glances at John, who still has the pistol pointing at him. 'So come on, I need to know why you are siding with this German rather than your comrade whom you have fought with'. He pauses for a few seconds, then glances at his fellow private. 'It is very complicated'. Private Walsh smirks and then shouts, 'Try me, John. You owe me that much'. Meanwhile, Hans looks extremely uncomfortable. He looks at his friend. 'Don't do it, John. Just kill him; then we can go our separate ways. As we have already said, no one will ever know'. He pauses again and then shakes his head. 'No Hans. Private Walsh is quite correct in what he is saying. He has every right to know'. Private Walsh gives him a look of frustration and then yells, 'Go on then. Enlighten me'. He looks at Hans (who shakes his head) and then his fellow private. 'Well ...'

John and Hans are sitting at the table as Peter and Harriet enter the kitchen.

Peter looks at the boys. 'Are you two sure that you do not want to come to the pub with us? Thomas and Olive will be pleased to see you both'. John shakes his head. 'No thanks, dad; we are going to stay in and have a game of chess. I am determined to beat Hans at least once before the Christmas period is over'. His father smiles. 'Are you both sure? We do not mind you both coming with us.' John shakes his head, 'No, honestly, we are happy playing chess and having a glass of wine'. He nods. 'Alright, as long as you both are sure'. He then looks at his wife. 'Come on, love, we had better get going. Otherwise, we will be late'. Harriet nods, then looks at her son. 'If you get hungry, there is plenty of food in the pantry. Just help yourselves'. He smiles. 'Do not worry, mam, we will be fine. Honest'. Peter looks at his watch, then his wife. 'Come on dear. We have to go. The boys will be all right. They are not children any more, you know'. She nods as her husband and looks at the pair. 'Enjoy yourselves. We will be back around ten'. John smiles. 'All right, dad, you better get going. Have a good time. Tell Thomas and Olive that we were asking after them both'. He smiles in his son's direction. 'I will do. See you both later. Enjoy your game'. With that, they leave the kitchen.

Once he has heard the front door shut, John looks at Hans before holding his hand. 'I thought they were never going to go'. Hans then leans across the table and kisses him passionately, who responds with equal passion. After they have stopped, John looks at his lover and suggests, 'Come on. Let's go upstairs. I have been thinking about this all day'. His lover nods. 'So, have I. I cannot wait to get you into bed'. John smiles, 'I am getting aroused at the thought'. The pair stand up and then head towards the kitchen door, hand in hand.

Returning to the barn loft, Private Walsh has a look of utter disgust on his face. He glares at John and shouts, 'You two are a couple of queers. It is my duty to take him prisoner and place you under arrest. You will be chucked out of the army in disgrace for this'. He goes for his rifle. John stares at him. 'I would not do that if I were you private'. He then pauses for a few seconds prior to continuing. 'I thought I could trust you if I told you the full story.' He shakes his head. 'It is just not normal. I have to do what I think is right'. John looks at his former comrade. 'You could just let Hans go, and that would be the end of it. As we have said many times now, no one would ever know. Private Walsh again shakes his head and once more shouts, 'No! I am taking your boyfriend prisoner and placing you under arrest'. He again goes for his rifle.

Without hesitation, Hans grabs the pistol and points it at the private. He then pulls the trigger, and there is a loud BANG. With that, the soldier drops to the ground and is motionless.

After a few seconds, Hans looks at his lover. 'I could not let you kill your fellow countryman

and comrade, so I did it instead. I had no choice'.
John has a look of utter shock on his face. 'You
were certainly ruthless. He did not stand a chance'
The German nods. 'Sometimes you have to be.
Look, if you think about it, you gave him every
opportunity to get out of this in a way that would
have been suitable to us all. Plus, all three of us
would have been alive. He decided not to take that
opportunity. That was his decision. Not ours.
Remember that'. He reluctantly nods. 'I suppose
you are right, but the guilt of what we did here
today will live with me for the rest of my life.
During our journey to get here, he told me things
about what happened to him when he was young;
really personal things. I will never forgive myself
for the part I played in this. He is right; I betrayed
him. But I was in an impossible position'. His
lover pauses for several seconds. 'It will ease in
time, I promise. Just remember, you did not shoot
him or indeed tell me to do it. I did it of my own
volition. I had no other option. You would have
been thrown out of the army and arrested for being
homosexual, like he said. I could not have that for
you'. He once again reluctantly nods his head in
agreement but does not say a single word as he
stares at Private Walsh's lifeless body.

Chapter Twenty-Five

Not far away from the barn, the sergeant glances at the two privates. 'I am sure that I just heard a shot, quite a way in the distance'. He then looks at Private Wright. 'Have a look and try to find out where it came from'. He nods. 'Yes, Sir'. He then salutes his commanding officer and then sets off in the direction from which the shot came.

Further back, Private Werner looks at his comrade. 'I think I heard a shot in the distance. 'Come on, let's get going. We do not want to be caught out in the open. They run in the direction of the shot.

Back at the barn loft, John asks his lover, 'So, how did you end up here?' 'I was sent behind enemy lines to try and gather some intelligence regarding British troop movements. Before I found anything out, I ran into those three unfortunate soldiers. After I killed the one who was lying in the barn, I captured the other two. I was going to leave them here alive and then head back to the German lines once it got dark. Unfortunately, all that changed when you and your comrades turned up'. Once again, John nods without uttering a word.

In the meantime, Private Wright cautiously

continues his journey towards the barn.

At the same time, the sergeant and Private Carter continue their journey. Not far behind them, the faint sound of footsteps can be detected. Private Carter looks at his companion. 'I think I heard something, Sir'. He glances at him and nods. 'Yes, so did I. Come on, we need to find some cover, and quickly'. He looks around. 'There is a bit of a wall over there. Let's head for that'. 'Good idea, private'. Without saying anything else, the pair quickly head towards the wall.

Meanwhile, Privates Werner and Braun continue their trek in the direction of the barn. Private Werner looks at his comrade. 'There are definitely some enemy soldiers in this area. I can feel it in my bones'. His fellow German nods and then points straight ahead. 'I can see a wall in the distance. Maybe we should head for that'. 'Yeah, at least there will be some cover if we manage to get there in one piece'.

Chapter Twenty-Six

Back at the barn loft, John briefly touches Hans' hand. 'You will need to be away from here by tomorrow, as they will come to collect the bodies. I will not be able to do anything to help you once that happens'. He smiles. 'Do not worry. I will be long gone and back behind my own lines by then'. His lover nods and then adds, 'Good. Hopefully, you will get back to your men safely'. 'I can only hope that this damned war will be over soon, and we will be in each other's arms again'. He smiles and then kisses him. Afterwards, he says, 'I also long for that day'. John senses his lover's arousal. He pulls him into the hay. Within seconds, both men are naked. John smiles as he climbs on top of his very excited sexual partner.

In the meantime, Private Carter looks over the wall and sees two German soldiers heading in his direction. He takes aim with his rifle.

There is a loud BANG, and Private Braun falls to the ground and does not move, and is clearly dead. Realizing this, Private Werner ignores him and runs as fast as he can towards the wall.

The sergeant sticks his head slightly above the wall and aims with his rifle.

Private Werner sees the head. He crouches down and takes aim with his rifle.

Back behind the wall, the sergeant's rifle jams. He shouts, 'Shi ...' Then there is another loud BANG, and he is hit in the head and is killed instantly. Within a few seconds, Private Carter carefully aims his rifle at the now-oncoming German soldier and fires.

There is yet another loud BANG, and Private Werner is hit in the arm. He falls to the ground.

Private Carter quickly reloads his rifle and takes aim. There is a fourth BANG. This time, Private Werner is hit in the leg and screams, 'Argh!' The private stares at the wounded German soldier. He quietly says to himself, 'Shit!'

At exactly the same time, whilst heading towards the barn, Private Wright hears gunshots. He stops running and pauses.

Back near the wall, Private Werner tries to stand up, but he quickly realizes that he can't. With no other option, he throws his rifle to the ground and shouts, 'I surrender!'

Chapter Twenty-Seven

At almost the same time, Private Wright is still standing in the middle of the track. He is deep in thought. After a few seconds, he shakes his head and starts to walk in the direction he was heading prior to stopping.

Meanwhile, behind the wall, Private Carter is unsure what to do.

He puts his rifle down and pauses to think.

Back at the barn loft, John and Hans are lying in each other's arms in the hay. John kisses his lover on the cheek. 'That was great'. 'Yes, it was'. John stands up and then glances at his still-naked partner. 'Come on, we need to get dressed. I need to go soon'. The German nods without adding to the conversation.

In the meantime, Private Carter picks up his rifle and takes aim at the German soldier and says to himself, 'I am sorry, but I cannot carry you back to our lines, and it would not be right to leave you here alone to bleed to death slowly'.

There is a final BANG. Private Werner is hit in the head. Blood spurts from the newly formed hole in his skull.

The British private shakes his head and quietly says to himself, 'May God forgive me'.

Still heading towards the barn, Private Wright ignores the next shot in the distance. He spots a farmer's field, pauses for a few seconds and then heads towards it.

A few seconds later, back at the battle site, Private Carter looks at the sergeant's body. 'I am so sorry you did not make it, Sir; I really am. It was an honor to go into battle with you'. He then goes through the sergeant's pockets. He quickly finds his ID and puts it into his own pocket, together with the letter for headquarters. He then comes out from behind the wall and heads towards the dead German soldier.

A couple of minutes later, Private Wright sees a barn in the distance and heads towards it.

At the same time, Private Carter, with his rifle poised, comes to the body of Private Werner. He glances at it. 'I am really sorry, soldier, but I had no choice. I could not leave you here to bleed to death. Rest in peace, whatever your name happens to be'.

After pausing for a few more seconds, he sets off in the direction Private Wright had gone earlier.

Chapter Twenty-Eight

In the meantime, Private Wright is still heading towards the barn.

Back at the barn loft, both John and Hans are now dressed. John looks in Private Walsh's pockets. He quickly finds his ID and puts it into his own pocket. He then does the same with the bodies of the two hostages. He then looks at his lover. 'Can you go into the barn and get Private White's ID for me? Private Walsh must have forgotten it earlier'. The German nods as John continues. 'Here, you might need this'. He then hands him the pistol. Hans tucks it into his belt. He puts his helmet on and then heads towards the ladder.

Private Carter continues to head in the same direction. He has his rifle poised.

About half a mile ahead, Private Wright approaches the barn. He notices that the door is open.

In the barn, Hans is going through Private White's pockets when he hears footsteps. He stops what he is doing and crouches down behind a bale of hay with his pistol poised.

A very nervous-looking Private Wright slowly
enters the barn with his rifle at the ready. He
quickly looks around and soon spots the body of the
dead British soldier.

Hans lifts his head just above the hay. He
spots the British soldier and immediately takes aim
with his pistol.

Private Wright sees the German soldier's
helmet behind the bale of hay. He quickly takes aim
with his rifle.

Hans fires his pistol.

There are two BANGS at precisely the same
time.

Hans is hit in the head and falls backwards.
Blood squirts from the wound, but he is still alive.
Only just.

Private Wright is hit in the heart. He is dead
before he even hits the ground.

Chapter Twenty-Nine

John hears the gunshots from the barn loft and, without hesitation, heads for the ladder.

At the same time, Private Carter hears the gunshots and runs towards the barn, which is now in sight.

John enters the barn. He looks around and sees the body of Private Wright. He then hears moaning coming from behind a bale of hay and quickly goes to investigate.

A few seconds later, he finds the badly wounded German and is visibly shocked. The extremely weak-looking Hans smiles at him; he then starts to shiver as he looks into his lover's eyes. 'I am really cold'. Blood begins to spurt from Hans' mouth as John holds his lover's hand. 'I love you. I always have. Ever since the day we first met'. Suddenly, he coughs and says, 'I love you ...' He then slumps backwards and dies.

Shortly after, John hears footsteps. He quickly steps away from the body of his now former lover and composes himself.

Chapter Thirty

Private Carter slowly enters the barn, with his rifle poised. Within a few seconds, he sees John. 'Are you alright? Where are the two soldiers you were with?' He glances at his fellow private. 'Yes, I am alright considering. Privates Walsh and White are both dead'. Private Carter shakes his head. 'What happened?'

He pauses for a few seconds to gather his thoughts. 'Private White was stabbed in a ditch by a German soldier. We brought him here, but he died later, and Private Walsh was shot by one of three German soldiers who were holding another two of our lads hostage. The Germans executed them. They also killed another of our lads who is over there'. The private again shakes his head, 'Jesus, you are lucky to be alive. We found the two dead Germans in the ditch and followed the trail of blood'. He nods. 'I am glad that you did, Benjamin'.

He pauses and then continues. 'For some reason, two of them left me with that one there'. He points at Hans' body. 'He was going to let me go, but then he heard Private Wright enter the barn. Unfortunately, they shot each other'. Again, he looks at his former lover's body. 'He was a good man. He tried to stop the executions. Anyway, what happened to you?' Private Carter pauses for a few seconds as if he is taking in what he has just heard. 'We were sent to find you and the other two. Once again, there were three of us. You know about Private Wright. The sergeant was killed in a gunfight with a couple of Germans about a mile away from here. John shakes his head. 'That is a pity as I really liked him. He was a decent man; as were all the others we knew who were killed'. His newly found comrade nods. 'I cannot argue with you there'. He then pauses. 'I wonder why they took hostages?' 'The German, they left me with, said they thought the two British lads had some intelligence that they needed. They certainly did not say anything whilst I was here. I know that for definite'. The private nods, then glances at John.

'I wonder why they did not kill you along with the others?' He looks at him. 'I think they would have. They just seemed more intent on leaving, as if they had to be somewhere else in a hurry. They told the soldier they left me with to 'sort it' and then catch them up'. Private Carter nods understandingly. 'So, in theory, they might return?' He shakes his head. 'They could come back. But somehow, I doubt it'. He glances at his fellow survivor. 'That might be true. But I do not want to be here if they decide to do so. One of us still needs to reach Headquarters. Do not forget'. John nods. 'I have not forgotten, private; I hid the letter in the loft. I will go and get it; then we can go.

Benjamin smiles. 'Fair enough'. Without saying anything else, John heads towards the ladder.

A few minutes later, John comes down the ladder with the letter in his hand. He looks visibly upset. Private Carter notices. 'Are you all right?' He quickly composes himself. 'Yes, I was just thinking of the men we lost: Privates Walsh, White and Wright, as well as the sergeant and the three others. What a waste of human life'. His comrade nods in agreement. 'It is sad, but that is war, I am afraid'. He half smiles. 'You are right. It does not make it any easier though'. He pauses for a few seconds and continues. 'Anyway, what are we going to do? I think we should attempt to make it through to headquarters, take the letter, get the reply and then head back to our lines'. His companion nods. 'That is fine by me'. He takes his copy of the letter from his pocket and glances at John. 'I have got a letter as well; I took it from the sergeant after he was killed. Apparently, it is the same as the one you have got'. John pauses for a few seconds and then advises, 'I think you should destroy it. If I get killed, you can take my copy. I do not think that we need two'. His new companion takes the letter from his pocket and proceeds to rip it up into tiny pieces. He then kicks the fragments all around the barn. He then looks at John. 'Right, that is done. No one will ever be able to put that back together. Not in a million years. I will just get Private Wright's ID, and then we can go'. He half smiles. 'I need to get

Private White's. I have already got the hostage's. Can you get the one from the lad lying near the entrance to the barn?' Benjamin nods and replies by saying, 'No problem. I will go and get it now'.

Five minutes later, the pair are ready to go. Private Carter hands his fellow private a rifle. 'I took it from that dead soldier. His name was Private Rice'. 'Thanks, Private Carter, sorry I meant Benjamin. Come on, let's go. There is nothing more we can do here. If we reach headquarters, we will inform the General about the bodies. Hopefully, he will arrange for them to be picked up'. Private Carter nods. Without saying another word, the pair head towards the barn door, leaving the dead soldiers behind them.

Chapter Thirty-One

Forty-five minutes later, the two privates are standing in front of General Robinson, who is sitting at his desk. John hands him the letter. He looks at the pair and shakes his head. 'You two look a bloody mess. What the hell happened to you both?' John glances at him and says, 'I will go first ...'

After they have finished regaling their stories, the general once again shakes his head. 'What a bloody waste of human life. If you both go and get something to eat from the mess, I will write a letter for you to take for your commanding officer. Come back in an hour, and it will be ready for you. Both men say in unison, 'Yes, Sir'. They then salute the general before heading towards the door'.

An hour later, the two privates enter the room and once again salute the general. He glances at the pair. 'Did you get enough to eat?' They both nod. John smiles and responds by saying, 'Yes, we did, Sir. Thanks for that'. He smirks, 'I did not bloody well cook it, private. I am not a master chef". The general then hands John a letter, which he puts into his top pocket. He then reveals, 'I have told your commanding officer to try and get the bodies of our lads picked up. Hopefully, this will happen. Make sure that you give him their ID's'. John glances at him. 'Yes, Sir, we will do. Thank you, Sir'. Both men salute the general and then leave.

Later in the day, John enters the officer's quarters back at the British trench. He is sitting at the table, staring at a map. John hands him the letter. He glares at him and says, 'You were a longtime private. I sent three more men to look for you. Where are Privates Walsh, White, Carter, Wright and the sergeant?' He pauses for a few seconds.
'Private Carter is outside speaking to a sergeant. Unfortunately, the rest of the men are all dead, Sir'. John then hands him all the ID's. The officer glances at them. He then picks three of them up. 'Who did these belong to?' He pauses for a few seconds. 'Well, Sir...'

After hearing his story, the officer shakes his head. 'Well done to you and Private Carter for getting through to headquarters, but it cost us four good men. What a bloody shame'. John nods in agreement. 'Yes Sir. It was. But we did our best in extremely difficult circumstances. 'I am sure you all did private'.

The officer then opens the letter and starts to read it. After he has finished, he reveals, 'Well, private, we are on our own. No reinforcements are forthcoming from headquarters. General Robinson also said that we should try to pick up the bodies tomorrow. John nods. 'Yes Sir. He said, Sir'. The officer looks at him. 'We will have to see what tomorrow brings; it is not like we can do anything for them now, is it?' He shakes his head. 'No, Sir'. He turns to leave, stops and then looks at the commanding officer before taking Private White's letters out of his pocket and continuing, 'Sorry, Sir. I almost forgot. Private White asked for these to be posted to his family before he died. He hands them to him. He glances at him and states, 'I will make sure his family gets them private. You have my word'. He nods in the officer's direction, salutes and then adds, 'Thank you for that, Sir. He was dying when he handed the letters over. He was upset that he wouldn't be able to see his baby son. It was very sad, to be honest'. 'I am sure it was private. Unfortunately, I have to think of the living, not the dead. That might sound harsh, but it is true. He then returns to looking at his map. Without saying another word. A clearly shocked John salutes him and then heads back towards the trench.

Chapter Thirty-Two

At 10.00 am on 11th November 1918, the officer calls all his men, including John, together and reveals, 'I have been asked to read you all this communication from headquarters'. Straight away, there is a silence.

He then proceeds to read from a prepared message, which he retrieves from his top pocket. It states, 'From 11.00 am today, all hostilities will cease. The Germans have surrendered'. All the men cheer. After they have gone quiet, the officer continues. 'So, all you have to do is keep your heads down for another hour. Then you all can go home'. He then puts the message back into his top pocket. The men cheer again as John walks away from the crowd. A single tear rolls down his cheek as he recalls his time with Hans …

John's room door is open as he unpacks his things. He spots Hans entering the room next door carrying a large suitcase. He looks at him with a smile on his face. 'You must be John, my new neighbor?' John stops what he is doing and turns towards him. He smiles back at his fellow student, who stares at him for just a bit too long. John notices and blushes slightly before composing himself. He glances at the man in front of him and asks, 'Hans?' The German nods. John goes out into the corridor and shakes his newfound friend's hand as he continues. 'Good to meet you, Hans'. His neighbor smiles and then replies. 'I am very pleased to meet you too'.

John looks at Hans as they stroll through the Keiser Wilhelm Park. He briefly touches Hans' hand. 'This is a beautiful place. You are very lucky to live so close to it'. The German smiles. 'Yes, it is and indeed I am. I actually came to the park's opening back in 1906 with my parents. It was actually designed by Walter Von Engelhardt. Interestingly, according to local records, which I have checked, part of the area that is now the park was a slaughterhouse in the late 1870s'. John shakes his head. 'You certainly know your local history, Hans.' He nods. 'Of course I do. It is something I have always been interested in. That is why I chose it as my degree subject at Cambridge'. The German then glances at his friend before continuing. 'Come on. We had better get back. My parents are going out tonight'. He nods. 'No problem at all'.

Shortly after, John is sitting at the table with Hans and his parents, Hans Senior and Gertrude. Four empty plates and four sets of cutlery are neatly stacked in the corner of the table.

Hans Senior looks at John. 'So, have you enjoyed your stay here in Dusseldorf?' He smiles.

'Yes, very much so, Hans. I am really grateful to you both for letting me stay here'. Hans Senior waves his hands dismissively. 'No problem at all. You are welcome here anytime'. 'Thank you for that; I am extremely grateful'. He nods, gets up from the table and looks at his wife. 'Come on, Gertrude. We had better get changed. Your sister will be expecting us for our weekly card game soon'. She gets up from the table but does not utter a single word.

John and Hans are sitting at the table as Peter and Harriet enter the kitchen.

Peter looks at the boys. 'Are you two sure that you do not want to come to the pub with us? Thomas and Olive will be pleased to see you both'. John shakes his head. 'No thanks, dad; we are going to stay in and have a game of chess. I am determined to beat Hans at least once before the Christmas period is over'. His father smiles. 'Are you both sure? We do not mind you both coming with us at all.' John shakes his head. 'No, honestly, we are happy playing chess and having a glass of wine'. He nods. 'Alright, as long as you both are sure'. He then looks at his wife. 'Come on, love, we had better get going. Otherwise, we will be late'. Harriet nods, then looks at her son. 'If you get hungry, there is plenty of food in the pantry. Just help yourselves'. He smiles. 'Do not worry, mam, we will be fine. Honest'. Peter looks at his watch, then his wife. 'Come on dear. We have to go. The boys will be all right. They are not children any more, you know'. She nods as her husband looks at the pair. 'Enjoy yourselves. We will be back around ten'. John smiles. 'All right, dad, you better get going. Have a good time. Tell Thomas and Olive that we were asking after them both'. He smiles in his son's direction. 'I will do. See you both later. Enjoy your game'. With that, they leave the kitchen.

Once he has heard the front door shut, John looks at Hans before holding his hand. 'I thought they were never going to go'. Hans then leans across the table and kisses him passionately; he responds with equal passion. After they have stopped, John looks at his lover and suggests, 'Come on. Let's go upstairs. I have been thinking about this all day'. His lover nods. 'So, have I. I cannot wait to get you into bed'. John smiles, 'I am getting aroused at the thought'. The pair stand up and then head towards the kitchen door, hand in hand.

The year is 1912, and several students rush in different directions on the Cambridge University campus to reach the results board.

John is carrying his books under his arm while trying (with great difficulty) to negotiate the throng. Amongst the sheer number of people, he spots Hans and quickly heads towards him.

Once he is close enough to him, he taps him on the shoulder. 'Hello, Hans. It will take ages to get close enough to see the board. I will come back when it's quieter, as it's pointless at the moment. I was wondering if you fancy a beer tonight? Hopefully, we can both celebrate getting our degrees together'. Hans nods. 'Yeah, I agree. I am coming back at lunchtime too. Do you fancy meeting then and getting our results? John smiles. We can also firm up our plans to go to the pub. 'Good idea. I will see you back here at lunchtime'. The German nods. John briefly touches his hand as they part.

John enters the barn. He looks around and sees the body of Private Wright. He then hears moaning coming from behind a bale of hay and quickly goes to investigate.

A few seconds later, he finds the badly wounded German and is visibly shocked. The extremely weak-looking Hans smiles at him; he then starts to shiver as he looks into his lover's eyes. 'I am really cold'. Blood begins to spurt from Hans' mouth as John holds his lover's hand. 'I love you. I always have. Ever since the day we first met'. Suddenly, he coughs and says, 'I love you ...' He then slumps backwards and dies.

Back to the present, Private Carter joins John and asks, 'Are you all right?' He nods. 'Yes. I was thinking back to that day, that is all', 'You have to look forward, not backwards, my friend. John half smiles and then says, 'You are right, Benjamin, but it does not stop me thinking about our brave comrades who died that day. I suppose I will have to come to terms with it, eventually'. He briefly touches John's hand and looks at him for a second longer than he should. 'If you want, we can meet up when we get back to Darlington'. He smiles. 'I would like that Benjamin'.

The pair then head towards where the other men are.

As they get closer to their comrades, the sound of the cheering grows louder.

PART II

Chapter One

Fast forward to 1933, and John shakes his head as he sits at the family's new kitchen table, reading a newspaper with his father. The headline reads: 'Adolf Hitler becomes Germany's new Chancellor'. He looks up at Peter. 'I have an awful feeling that this is not going to end well, dad'. He nods in agreement. 'I think you could be right. He needs stopping'. John lets out a huge sigh. 'I agree, but by whom?' His father smiles. 'That is the question everyone wants the answer to. No one wants another war, so the major countries will hope that it just goes away. Their answer is to sweep it under the carpet, and then, in their minds, the problem has gone away'. John pauses for a few seconds. 'What about the League of Nations? Surely, they can do something? As that is what they were set up for after the last war'. Peter shakes his head. 'No, no, they would not do anything because they are too weak'. John nods without uttering another word but continues to stare at the newspaper headline.

It is now 1938, and gangs of SS men and women, including Gertrude, smash up Jewish shops in Berlin. Windows are put through, and the aforementioned shops are looted. She looks at her cohorts and yells, 'Come on. Let's burn their businesses down. We should have done it years ago'. She then sets fire to a piece of paper with a cigarette lighter and throws it into a shop doorway.

She grins with satisfaction as she watches the fire take hold and then laughs out loud. After a few seconds, she heads up the street towards the next shop in the row of five.

A little later, after looting another shop, Gertrude spots a Jewish man hiding in an alleyway. She goes up to him and, without a second thought, gleefully takes her revolver out of its holster and shoots him in the head before shouting, 'That is what you get for being a dirty, money-grabbing Jewish pig. The same thing will happen to you all. Mark my words'. She then smirks before kicking the now lifeless body into the gutter and then walking away from it, laughing out loudly, once more. She stops, turns around and looks at the body. 'At least you will not be stealing from us Germans anymore, you dirty piece of shit'. Gertrude then continues her trip up the street, still laughing out very loudly.

The following year, British Prime Minister Neville Chamberlain steps off an airplane with an agreement he signed with Adolf Hitler in his hand. He addresses the assembled crowd and reveals, 'This morning I had another talk with the German Chancellor, Herr Hitler, and here is the paper which bears his name upon it as well as mine. Some of you, perhaps, have already heard what it contains, but I would just like to read it to you. Mr. Chamberlain pauses. He then starts to read the statement. 'We, the German Fuhrer and Chancellor, and the British Prime Minister, have had a further meeting today and are agreed in recognizing that the question of Anglo-German relations is of the first importance for the two countries and for Europe. We regard the agreement signed last night and the Anglo-German Naval Agreement as symbolic of the desire of our two peoples never to go to war with one another again. We are resolved that the method of consultation shall be the method adopted to deal with any other questions that may concern our two countries, and we are determined to continue our efforts to remove possible sources of difference, and thus to contribute to assure the peace of Europe'.

Later, outside number 10 Downing Street, Mr. Chamberlain reads the following statement:

'My good friends, for the second time in our history, a British Prime Minister has returned from Germany, bringing peace with honor. I believe it is peace for our time. Go home and get a nice, quiet sleep'.

Chapter Two

In August 1939, John is sitting at the kitchen table reading a book when he hears a knock at his front door. He puts the book down, gets up, and then leaves the room.

A few seconds later, he opens the door, and a short man is standing in front of him. He smiles. 'Hello. I am looking for a John Wray'. John looks puzzled. 'Why may I ask?' The man smiles once more. 'I have something of the utmost importance that I need to speak to him about'. He returns the smile. 'I am John Wray'. The man glances at him. May I come in?' He pauses for a few seconds, then opens the door wider and beckons the man to enter. 'Yes. Of course, you can'.

Within a couple of minutes, John is sitting in an easy chair in the living room. The man is sitting opposite. He looks at him. 'I am Tony Garbutt'. He then holds his hand out towards his host, who shakes it. 'Good to meet you, Tony. Now, what is so important for you to want to come and see me?' He smiles and then pauses. 'What I am about to tell you is strictly between the two of us. It must not go any further'. John nods. After which Tony shows him his ID, John looks at it before Tony puts it back into his inside jacket pocket. John confirms from the ID that his guest is from MI5. He then looks at him with a smirk on his face. 'Is this some sort of prank? I really do not have time for this as I

have to be elsewhere within the next thirty minutes. Additionally, I am not in the mood for jokes. His visitor shakes his head. 'I am also an incredibly busy man, particularly now with everything that is going on in the world at the moment. I certainly would not travel by train from London to Darlington to play a joke on you. I have far better things to do with my time, of that I can assure you, dear boy'. John nods in agreement. 'Alright. Fair enough. I am sorry. However, you have to understand, it does seem a bit strange to have someone from MI5 knocking at your door'. Tony smiles. 'Yes, in fairness, it does, but I can assure you that I am who I say I am. You can ring MI5 if you want, and they will confirm after you give them a password, which I will supply to you, that I am a part of that organization'. He shakes his head. 'No, no, I believe you'. Tony nods. 'Good, the thing is, we need your help. You are the perfect person for the job that we need carrying out'. John has a puzzled look on his face. 'How is that?' The MI5 agent smiles. 'You are a journalist, and in addition, you speak very good German'. He looks surprised. 'How do you know so much about me?' Tony grins. 'We did a thorough background check on you. We have to'. He gives him a questioning look. 'So, that is all well and good, but what do you want me to do?' He pauses for what seems like an eternity and then glances at him. 'We need you to go to Berlin and report back to us what is happening there'. John also pauses, and once again, he has a puzzled look on his face. 'Do you mean spy? Surely you have other people over there who could do this kind of job for you?' He nods. 'Yes, indeed I do. However, the reason why you are perfect for the assignment is that you are actually a journalist. So, if the Germans happen to check up on you, they will be able to confirm that this is indeed the case'. John nods as his guest continues. 'You will be providing your country with great service, dear boy. However, if you do not want to get involved, I will accept that and walk away, and nothing else will ever be said, and you will never see or hear from me again'. John then looks at him. 'And if I decide to help?' His guest pauses again. 'You will be given a briefing in London before you leave for Berlin'. He looks at his visitor questioningly. 'What about my day job?' Tony smiles. 'We will sort that, trust me; it would not be a problem at all. So do not worry about that. You have my word that your job will still be there for you to carry on with when you return from Berlin'. John once again pauses for a couple of seconds. 'Sorry for asking so many questions, but how long do I have to make up my mind, one way or another?' The agent glances at him. 'Do not worry about it. I fully understand that you need to know all the facts before making your decision'. I will be back tomorrow and need a definite answer, one way or the other. In the meantime, as I touched on earlier, do not mention this to a soul, not even your parents'. He nods. 'Do not worry; I will not say a word to anyone. You have my word'. Tony smiles. 'Good lad; until tomorrow, dear boy'. He shakes John's hand, gets up, and heads towards the door.

Later that night, John is lying in bed. He goes over the conversation with Tony. One part of it goes through his mind over and over again. 'You will be providing your country with a great service'. After pausing for a few seconds, he says to himself, 'I think you are going to have to do this, John. Really, you have no choice'.

The following morning, Tony once again sits opposite John, this time at the kitchen table. He looks at him questioningly. 'Have you come to a decision, dear boy?' He nods. 'I have decided to do it as I feel in my own mind that it is the right thing to do'. Tony smiles and then shakes his hand. 'That is fantastic, absolutely fantastic. I am really pleased to have you onboard'. He glances at his new colleague. 'When do you want me to come to London?' The agent smiles in his direction. 'The day after tomorrow, then we will brief you and then off to Berlin you go'.

Chapter Three

Two days later, John is sitting at a desk at MI5 opposite Tony. The MI5 agent pushes a file to one side. 'That is all your paperwork sorted'. He then hands him a fake ID, which he takes from his inside jacket pocket. 'If you get compromised, use this ID. Do not tell anyone that you have this, not anyone at all. And I really mean that, dear boy; it is vitally important'. John nods. He then puts it into his own inside jacket pocket.

Just then, there is a knock at the door. Tony looks up and shouts loudly, 'Come in'. A middle-aged man enters the room. John looks shocked as he looks at the man. 'David, what are you doing here? I thought you would be at work'. Tony looks at him. 'As well as being your boss at the Northern Echo, David also works for us and has done so for several years. The newspaper editor looks at him. 'It was I who recommended you for this job. You will be perfect for it'. Tony smiles and confirms, 'Indeed, it was. And he will give you all the information you need. Your cover is perfect, so you should not be in any danger at all, as long as you are careful and do exactly what he advises you to do'.

Shortly after, John is stood in David's office. The agent, who is sitting at the desk, hands him a pistol, which he takes from his top drawer. 'You will need to keep this really well concealed'.

He nods. David then stands up and retrieves a
suitcase from behind his desk. 'You will also need
to take this with you. It has a secret compartment.
There is extra ammunition hidden in it, which is at
the bottom of the case'. He nods. 'It sounds like
you have thought of everything'. He smiles. 'We
try our best, John. Your contact in Berlin is Paul,
one of our best agents. He is expecting you.' He
then opens his bottom desk drawer, takes out a
photograph, and shows it to him. 'This is Paul.
When you first meet him, you must say that you are
The Northern Echo reporter'. John nods. After
putting the photograph back into the drawer from
his jacket pocket, he then hands John a piece of
paper. 'This is the address in Berlin where you
have to meet Paul. Please memories it and then
destroy it. We cannot risk it getting into the wrong
hands'. He puts the paper into his pocket. 'No
problem. When do I leave?' David glances at him.
'Tomorrow morning. I have already informed the
staff at the paper that you will be covering a story
in Berlin, so there is no need to worry about that.
He nods as his boss continues. 'One final piece of
advice: if things get too hot over there, get out, do
not take any risks, none at all. We want you back at
the paper in one piece'. He smiles, then nods. 'All
right, I will certainly bear that in mind'. David
smiles. 'Good. All that remains is for me to wish
you good luck'. He then shakes his boss's hand
before announcing, 'Thanks. I will not let you
down. I promise you'. 'I know you would not do
that. That is why I recommended you for this
assignment in the first place'. He smiles as David

glances at him. 'Oh, I nearly forgot your flight tickets'. He takes them from his middle desk drawer and hands them to him before saying, 'You would not get far without these'. He nods. 'Yes, that would have been a bit of a nightmare, to say the least'. He smiles and ends the conversation by saying, 'Indeed, it would. Like I said earlier, Good luck. I am sure that you will be fine'. John pauses for a few seconds, takes a letter out of his jacket pocket and hands it to his editor. 'If anything happens to me, will you please ensure my parents get this?' He nods and then puts it into his top desk drawer. 'Nothing will happen to you. It is a straightforward mission'. John nods. 'I know that, but I just wanted to cover all of the angles. You know what I am like'. David smiles. 'Indeed, I do. I will return it to you when you get back'. He pauses for a few seconds. 'Good idea'. I look forward to tearing it up'. He pauses and then continues. 'Anyway, I will get going; many thanks for putting your trust in me to do this job'. David smiles for the final time. 'I look forward to having a few drinks with you in Darlington when you get back. I might even come to a Darlington match with you'. He nods. 'I will hold you to that David. It is about time you met my dad'. He then shakes his boss's hand before heading towards the door.

The next day, back in Darlington, John is finishing packing his suitcase on his bed. He ensures that he has put the fake ID and the pistol into the secret compartment and zipped it up before getting up and taking a last look around the room to

ensure that he has not forgotten anything. John
then heads towards the door with a slightly worried
look on his face.

A few minutes later, he is sitting opposite his
parents at the kitchen table. He looks at them both.
'I have got something very important to tell you'.
He then pauses for a few seconds before
continuing. 'I am been sent to Berlin by the paper
for a short time to do a story for them'. Both of his
parents look really concerned. Peter glances at his
son. 'It looks like we could be at war with
Germany any day now. I would think carefully
before you accept this assignment'. He looks at his
father. 'I will be there and back long before
anything happens. In addition, I have already
agreed to do it, as no one else would even consider
it'. Harriet briefly touches his hand. 'I am not
surprised! That aside, we worry about you son'. He
smiles. 'Honestly, I will be fine, mam. It is a
straightforward job. As I said earlier, I will be back
before you know it'. Unseen by John but seen by
his mother, Peter's facial expression tells a totally
different story.

The following morning, John is stood on the
footpath outside his parent's house. They are both
stood on the doorstep facing him. Harriet looks at
her son. 'It only seems like yesterday that we saw
you off to fight in the Great War back in 1914.
Now it seems like we are doing it all over again'.
He shakes his head. 'Mam, it is totally different this
time. I will be fine. Honest'. She hugs him, and

then Peter shakes his hand. 'Have a safe journey and for God's sake, be careful'. John smiles and then nods his head. 'I will, mam. You have my word'.

As John walks down the street, a single tear rolls down his mother's face.

At the same time, Peter holds his wife's hand tightly. 'He is a clever lad, Harriet; he will be fine.' She looks at her husband with a stern look on her face. 'That is not what your expression told me yesterday. I saw you know. Luckily, John did not see it.' He is shocked at the revelation but does not utter another word as the pair step back inside their house and close the front door behind them.

Chapter Four

Later that day, John stands outside Paul's house in Berlin. After pausing for a few seconds, he knocks on the front door. Within a minute, the agent is standing on the doorstep in front of him. John smiles at him. 'Hi. I am John, the reporter from the Northern Echo. You were expecting me?' He nods, looks in both directions and then quickly ushers him inside.

Shortly after, the pair enter the living room. John looks around. The room is extremely sparsely furnished, with only a table, two chairs and two armchairs. There is also an old rug near the fireplace. The MI5 Operative looks at his guest. 'I am Paul. Good to meet you'. He holds out his hand and then shakes it. 'Good to meet you too'. Paul points to one of the armchairs. 'Take a seat'. John does as he is asked, and then Paul continues. 'Tony mentioned a few details as to why you are here'. He nods. 'Yes, I have to find out what is going on, do a story to complete my cover, and then get out of Germany'. The agent smiles. 'I know. Tony told me that much'. John looks at his host. 'Anyway, if you do not mind, I thought I would go for a look around to get a feel for the place'. Paul has a worried look on his face. John notices. 'Don't worry, I will be fine'.

Twenty minutes later, John is walking up the street when he is stopped by an SS officer who asks (in German), 'Papiere bitte' ('Papers please'). He takes his ID from his inside coat pocket and hands it to the officer, who checks it and then returns it to him before enquiring in English, 'So, what are you doing here in Berlin, my friend?' John puts the ID back into his pocket. 'I work for a newspaper in England, and with Adolf Hitler signing a peace treaty with Britain, we wanted to write a story about how life has changed for the better in Germany'. He then pauses before continuing. 'If I may say so, you speak excellent English'. The German smiles and then nods before revealing, 'Yes. I spent a lot of time in the South of England when I was younger. It is a beautiful country'. He pauses for a few seconds and then continues. 'I will give you a piece of advice: do not speak to the Jews; they spread lies, and you want your story to be truthful, don't you?'. He nods. 'Thank you for that information. I will certainly bear it in mind'. The SS Officer nods. 'You can go now. Enjoy your stay here in Berlin'. John smiles and then starts to walk away.

Shortly after, John hears shouting. He goes to the street corner and watches what is happening with great interest.

The SS officer, whom he had just been talking to, glares at a male Jew who is trying to get past him. He then yells, 'You should walk in the gutter, you filthy Jewish pig'. He then punches him hard in the stomach, and he falls to the ground. The German then follows up with several blows to both

the head and the body. He is left writhing in agony
on the road. John shakes his head in disbelief as he
watches the proceedings progress. The SS officer
looks at the Jew with pure hate. 'Do not forget next
time, you filthy piece of shit'. He then gives the
man two more kicks in the stomach for good
measure before walking away, laughing out loudly
to himself.

Once the SS officer has left, John helps
the man to his feet. He smiles. 'Thank you, Sir'.
John looks at him in disbelief. 'It is really bad what
is happening here'. The Jew nods. 'Indeed, it is.
Anyway, you had better go. If they catch you
talking to me, they will arrest you on the spot'.
John takes his wallet from his pocket and quickly
removes twenty Marks and hands it to the man in
front of him. 'Here, take this. I only wish that I
could do more for you'. He very carefully puts the
money into his pocket and then smiles. 'Thank you
for this. It is the first act of kindness anyone has
shown me in a long, long time, and I shall not
forget it. Now go before anyone sees you talking to
me'. 'All right. Good luck, my friend'. The Jew
looks at him. 'Same to you, and thank you for the
money. It will feed my family for a couple of days
at least'. Before he can say anything else, the man
has started to walk away in the other direction.

John continues to wander around the city
center, mentally taking notes of what is going on.
In one instance, he sees several Hitler Youth Boys
picking on a Jewish boy aged no more than nine.

They kick him to the ground and throw the bag he
was carrying into the road. It is then run over by an
oncoming lorry. The Hitler Youth boys laugh.
Passers-by ignore the boys' plight and go about
their daily business. An elderly man goes towards
the frightened boy, who is now lying bleeding in
the road. He then sees the Hitler Youth Boys,
pauses for a couple of seconds, and then quickly
changes his mind and scuttles off in the other
direction. John is clearly shocked and says quietly
to himself, 'What the hell is going on in this
country? It has changed beyond recognition since I
came here with Hans, not really that long ago. He
would be turning in his grave if he knew what was
going on now in the country he loved. I wonder
what his parents think. Especially Hans Senior'.

Shortly after, he walks up a side street. He
stops outside many former Jewish shops, most of
which have been boarded up. He shakes his head
as he sees the anti-Jewish slogans scrawled all over
the previously mentioned shop doors and walls. His
facial expression shows that he is clearly moved by
what he has just witnessed. Once again, he says to
himself, 'I find the whole of this really sad. It is
certainly not the Germany I loved anymore'. He
then turns and heads back in the direction of the
house where he is staying.

Twenty minutes later, he is about to enter
Paul's house when he hears a noise coming from
inside, followed by a gunshot. Without hesitating,
he very quickly runs away from the scene.

Chapter Five

After waiting for a while to gather his thoughts, John enters the house and listens for any movement coming from any of the rooms. When he is certain that there is not any, he heads towards the living room door.

When he enters, he sees Paul on the floor with a gunshot wound to his stomach. He moves and then grabs John's arm. 'It looks like you have been compromised. The SS are coming back for you'. He is shocked as the MI5 Operative continues. 'I told them that you have not arrived yet. They left to try and find you'. John looks at him. 'Is there anything I can do for you?' He shakes his head. 'No. I am finished. But listen, I have to tell you something very important'. He briefly glances at the stricken agent. 'What is that?' He once again briefly touches John's arm. 'MI5 used you to flush David out. He is a double agent. Do not contact him under any circumstances; contact Tony'. He shakes his head. 'I do not believe it. I have known him for years'. Paul glares at a clearly shocked John. 'It is true. You must leave here and from now on, use your fake ID'. 'What about you?' Paul shakes his head. 'Forget about me. Contact Joe; he will help you'. John has a puzzled look on his face. 'Joe?' The agent nods weakly. 'Yes, his details are in the bedroom, along

with your things. You must get out of Germany as
fast as possible, with or without Joe'. He glances
at the agent's wound. 'Can I make you more
comfortable?' He once again shakes his head.
'There is no time for that. You must leave as soon
as possible, because they will definitely come back
for you, as they said they would. He nods and then
quickly heads towards the bedroom.

Fifteen seconds later, he enters and looks
around. He cannot see his possessions, so he rushes
back towards the living room.

Once there, he approaches the MI5 agent.
'Paul, where are my things?' He is now visibly
weaker and whispers, 'If you lift the carpet up, you
will find them. Joe's address is also there. His
password is 'Manchester United'. He breathes
heavily and then dies. John closes the agent's eyes
and then pauses for a second before heading back
to the bedroom.

On entering, he quickly lifts up the carpet. In
the middle of the room, he sees a trapdoor. He
opens it and starts to climb down the steps.

Once he is in the cellar, his eyes take a while
to adjust to the poor light. Eventually, he spots a
switch on the wall and turns the light on. He
quickly notices his suitcase in the corner and heads
towards it. He opens it and takes the pistol and ID
out of the secret compartment. John then scans the

room and spots a pistol silencer, which is on a
shelf. He goes over to it and picks it up, together
with a notebook next to it. He quickly scans
through the pages, finds Joe's address and tears it
out. He pauses for a few seconds, shakes his head,
and then decides to put the whole notebook into his
trouser pocket, together with the page he tore out.
John also puts the pistol into his coat pocket and
the ID into his inside jacket pocket. Just then, he
hears a noise from above and then voices coming
from the living room. He quickly runs up the steps.

Once he is safely in the bedroom, John
retrieves the pistol from his pocket and attaches the
silencer, which is still in his hand, before heading
towards the living room.

Through a gap in the living room door, he
sees two SS officers examining Paul's body.
Without hesitation, John aims at one of them with
his pistol and fires. He sees him fall to the floor and
does not move thereafter. The other German
panics, and before he can do anything, there is a
muted gunfire sound; he also drops to the floor and
like his former comrade, he is motionless.

Shortly after, John drags the body of one of
the SS officers and lays it next to his cohort in the
cellar. He scours the room and notices a blanket on
a shelf. He gets it down and throws it over the
corpses, and briefly glances at the covered bundles
before turning and heading towards the steps.

A minute later, he appears in the bedroom from the hatch. He puts the carpet back after he closes it, before looking around the room. After pausing for a few seconds, he moves the bed to cover the hatch. He also moves a wooden chest to where the bed was. Finally, he gets on his hands and knees and smooths the carpet as best he can. He quickly surveys his handiwork and smiles to himself before leaving the room.

A minute later, he enters the living room and glances at Paul's lifeless body. He whispers in his direction, 'I am sorry that I did not get to know you better, Paul. I am sure that we would have worked well together. Unfortunately, we will never know the answer to that now'. He then heads towards the door.

Chapter Six

Later that evening, John knocks on Joe's front door. The agent, a man in his forties, answers and looks at him. 'Who are you?' John smiles and reveals, 'I am John, Paul sent me'. He glances at him. 'Come in'.

The two men enter the living room. Suddenly, Joe goes to the cabinet and grabs a gun, which already has a silencer fitted. He points it at John. 'How do I know who you are?' He remains calm and reveals, 'Your password is 'Manchester United'. Joe puts the gun down and looks at him. 'I am sorry about that, but I had to be sure that you are who you say you are. Anyway, where is Paul?' John pauses for a couple of seconds. 'I am sorry to say, but he is dead. The SS shot him'. Joe is visibly upset and takes a few seconds to process what he has just been told. Eventually, he glances at John. 'How did you get away?' Once again, he pauses and then begins to regale his story. 'Well ...'

After he has heard the tale, Joe looks at his guest. 'You were fortunate, my friend'. He nods as the agent continues. 'If those SS officers had got back earlier, you would be a dead man, without a doubt'. 'I know that. Like you said, I was very lucky. I have been thinking, with what has happened, I really need to contact Tony to let him know that I have been compromised'. The agent looks at him. 'The house three doors up is now empty. An old man lived there, but he died suddenly'. John looks surprised. 'Did he not have any family?' Joe shakes his head. 'No, he did not have anyone, and no one ever visited when he was alive, or at least whilst I was his neighbor. And with everything that was going on, I easily disposed of his body and did not tell anyone. No one came looking for him, so after a couple of weeks, I put a radio in his house. You can contact Tony to update him on that. I will destroy it once you have done that. We can go and do that now if you want?' He nods. 'Yes, I think I should, to be honest'. With that, both men get up and head towards the door.

Ten minutes later, the pair enter Joe's former neighbor's living room. Joe heads straight towards the radio, which is hidden under a pile of clothes on the floor behind a settee, and hands it to his companion.

Within a few seconds, John is tapping away in Morse Code.

A few minutes later, Tony is sitting in an armchair in his lounge, reading a newspaper, when the telephone rings. He puts the paper on the chair arm, then gets up and heads towards the table where his telephone is situated. He picks up the receiver. He has a concerned look on his face as he listens to a voice on the other end of the telephone. He ends the call by saying, 'All right, many thanks for letting me know, dear boy. Do not forget, keep this to yourself, just like we discussed'.

Back at his former neighbor's house, Joe looks at his companion. 'What did you tell them? I could not keep up with you.' 'I told them what had happened and said we are heading to Switzerland'. Without hesitation, Joe picks up the radio, smashes it on the floor, and then looks at his fellow agent. 'We do not need it any more. So, we do not want it getting into the wrong hands, as I mentioned earlier'. John nods in agreement. 'Yes, I agree. It is much better to be safe than sorry'.

At precisely the same time, Tony is standing with the telephone receiver still in his hand. He replaces it and then picks it up again, and then he starts to dial a number. Within a minute, he says into it, 'Hi David. It is Tony. David, I need to speak to you tomorrow. It is of the utmost importance that I see you in person ... Yes, tomorrow afternoon will be fine ... It is nothing at all to worry about; I just need your help with something that has come up, and I need someone that I can rely on … Yes, see you then dear boy ... I look forward to it … Bye'. He then replaces the receiver and smiles to himself before saying, 'Got you at last, you bloody traitor. At least no one else will die because of you now. I only hope that John and Joe get out of Germany safely. If they don't, it will be on me'.

A few minutes later, John and Joe are sitting at the table in Joe's living room. John looks at the

MI5 Agent. 'It is a good idea to try and get to Switzerland'. He nods. 'Yes, we will head for the British Embassy there'. Just then, there is a knock on the door. Without hesitation, both men get their pistols out. Before they can do anything, they hear the front door burst open with some force. They each get up and crouch at the side of the settee with their pistols at the ready.

A few seconds later, three SS officers burst into the room. Both of the agents open fire. Two of the Germans drop to the floor and do not move. The third one gets a shot off and hits Joe in the head. He is clearly no longer alive. John fires at the last remaining German and hits him in the head. He falls to the floor and, once again, he does not move.

Shortly after, John checks to ensure there is no one else outside by looking through the window. He then heads over to Joe and quickly realizes that he is dead, so, therefore, nothing can be done for him. He says to himself, 'Two good agents dead since I arrived in Germany! Could I have done anything different?' He then shakes his head and adds, 'God knows. However, I have certainly let myself in for more than I originally thought. That is for sure'.

He hurriedly searches through the first SS officer's overcoat and finds some car keys in a pocket. He puts them into his own jacket pocket. After glancing at the former agent's body for a

couple of seconds and shaking his head, he leaves
the room.

Chapter Seven

A few hours later, John drives the car down a country road. After a few minutes, he pulls into a lay-by. He then picks up and looks at a map which had been left on the seat next to him. After finishing consulting it, he pulls the car back onto the road and resumes his journey.

The following morning, he pulls off the road and drives through a field into a wooded area. He stops the car and gets out to stretch his legs.

John scouts the area. He looks towards the way he has just driven and is happy that the car cannot be seen from the road. After pausing for a few seconds, he says to himself, 'I wonder what is up here? I suppose that there is only one way to find out'. He then decides to continue walking in the same direction.

After travelling for around twenty minutes, he comes across an isolated farmhouse. He goes up to the window and peers through it. There does not appear to be anyone at home. He then looks around. The area near the house seems to be deserted. After checking a couple more times, he tries the front door, and to his relief, he discovers it is open.

John enters the kitchen, looks through the cupboards, and quickly notices they are empty. He then spots a walk-in pantry and heads towards it.

Once inside, he spots some bread, cheese and biscuits on a shelf. He turns around, and behind the door, he sees a cloth bag that is hanging on a nail. He grabs it and quickly stuffs some of the bread and cheese into it, then turns to leave. On his return to the kitchen, he is confronted by a woman dressed in overalls and a shirt. She is standing directly in front of him. The woman stares at him. 'What are you doing in my house?' He looks startled. 'I was going to leave you some money for the food'. The woman looks at him. 'Are you on the run from the SS?' He nods. The woman points to a seat at the table. 'Sit down, if you do not mind'.

He pauses and then sits at the table opposite the woman, who glances at him. 'I am Sarah'. He smiles. 'Good to meet you, Sarah. I am John'. They shake hands. He then asks, 'Are you Jewish?' She is taken aback by the question. 'Why do you ask?' He reveals, 'I saw a Kippah hung up in the pantry'. She nods. 'It was my husband's'. He pauses for a few seconds. 'Where is he?' Sarah divulges, 'He is dead'. He shakes his head as the house owner continues. 'He went to Berlin six months ago to check up on his parents. He was beaten to death by Hitler Youth boys outside their house'. He sighs and then shakes his head. 'That is terrible'. I saw something similar when I was in Berlin myself. I was absolutely appalled'. She nods in agreement. 'In answer to your question, yes, I am Jewish'. He smiles. 'I am half Jewish, and I need to get out of the country'. 'Where are you heading?' He pauses for a few seconds. 'Firstly, Dusseldorf'. He takes some money out of his pocket and drops it on the table before continuing. 'For the food'. She pushes the money back towards him and suggests, 'You can stay here for a while if you want'. He shakes his head. 'Thanks for the offer, but I really have to be going'. He picks up the bag, then gets up to leave. 'I appreciate you letting me have this food. So, thanks again for that'. He then heads towards the door. Sarah glances at him. 'Where is your car?' 'About a mile up the road, I need to get back to it. Once again, many thanks for your help'. He shakes her hand and then leaves. She then picks the money up and puts it into her overall pocket.

Shortly after, John heads back in the direction of his parked car. He looks behind him, pauses and then hides behind a tree. He then gets his pistol out. Sarah passes the tree. He puts it back into the inside of his jacket, then grabs her from behind and wrestles her to the ground. He glares at her. 'Why did you follow me?' The clearly frightened Sarah discloses, 'I was curious, so I decided to see where you were parked'. He lets her go as she continues by asking, 'Can I come with you?' He looks at her questioningly. 'Why? You do not even know me'.

She glances at him and then states, 'I am lonely'. She then starts to undo her overalls. 'I will make it worth your while'. John shakes his head. 'I am not interested in the slightest'. She lets her overalls fall to the ground. Her shirt is undone, exposing her bare breasts, and her legs are also bare. She suggests, 'Maybe this will change your mind. If you stay, you can have me as often as you want'. He shakes his head again. 'Go home, Sarah. You are worth a hell of a lot more than allowing yourself to be used like that'. An evidently shocked and upset Sarah says, 'But most men would jump at that chance'. However, he turns and walks away. He then stops and glances at her. 'As I said, go back home. Plus, I am not like most men'. She starts to put her overalls back on as he continues his journey back to his car, shaking his head in disbelief in the process.

Twenty minutes later, he is back in the wooded area. He gets into the car, starts the engine and then drives away.

At almost midnight, he pulls the car off the road and parks it behind a hedge, where it cannot be seen. He then gets out of the driver's seat and climbs into the back seat, where he tries to go to sleep.

The following morning, he wakes up, stretches, and then gets out of the car. He walks over to a tree and urinates against it. He is interrupted when he hears the sound of another car coming in his direction, some distance away. He quickly buttons himself up and then heads back to the car, which is parked near the tree.

Once he is back inside the car, he can hear the noise of the oncoming vehicle grow louder. The engine noise can then be heard at its loudest, and then it gradually fades. He breathes a sigh of relief as he starts up his own engine.

Later that evening, John drives past a signpost that says 'Dusseldorf 20 KM'. He stops the car out of sight from the roadway, gets out of the front seat once again, and gets into the bigger back seat and quickly falls asleep.

The following day, John is driving when he spots a signpost that reads, 'Dusseldorf 3 KM'. He pulls the car over to the side of the road and shuts off the engine. He pauses for a few seconds before restarting the car.

Shortly after, he is driving slowly up the road and spots a secluded lane. He drives up it. To the right, there is a wooded area. After stopping and pausing for a couple of seconds, he starts to move again, turns towards it, and continues his journey.

The car struggles to move on the rough ground as he drives deeper into the woods. He

stops, turns off the engine, and opens the door. He
gets out, stands beside the car, and scours the area.
John then begins to pick up some leaves and
branches up.

The car can no longer be seen within two
hours, as it is covered in the aforementioned leaves
and branches. He looks at it and says to himself,
'That was a job well done.' He then turns and walks
away from the wooded area, leaving the covered
car behind him.

Five minutes later, he comes across a very
steep embankment. He takes the car keys out of his
jacket pocket and throws them as far down it as he
can before smirking and then saying to himself,
'Good luck to anyone who is hoping to find them'.
He then continues his journey.

Chapter Eight

Two hours later, Hans Senior (from now on referred to as Hans in this story) and John are sitting at the table in Hans's kitchen. They each have a cup of coffee in front of them. Hans looks at his visitor. 'So, what brings you to Germany John?' He smiles. 'It is a long story'. 'We have all night'. He pauses for thought before declaring, 'I honestly do not know where to start'. Hans advises, 'Try the beginning. That is normally the best way'. Again, he pauses for a few seconds, then begins to tell his tale, 'It all started when I got a visit from this funny little man ...'

After hearing the story, Hans has a shocked look on his face. 'What are you planning to do?' He glances at the middle-aged man. 'I need to get to Switzerland. I have the feeling that there is going to be another war between our two countries'. Hans nods in agreement. 'I think you could be right'. He then looks at his companion before continuing. 'I will help you all I can. You know that, don't you? It is what Hans would have wanted'. He smiles. 'Yes, I thought that. That is why I knew I could rely on you, which is why I came here. By the way, where is Gertrude?' Hans pauses briefly. 'She is away with the SS. She will be back tomorrow evening'. John looks concerned as his host continues. 'I am going to have to hide you in the cellar until we decide what to do for the best'. John still has a worried look on his face as the German reveals, 'Gertrude is high up in the SS now; she hates Jews

and would not hesitate to tell them that you were
here. For some reason, she blames them for Hans
dying, which is absolutely crazy'.

He thinks back to his last moments in the
barn with Hans …

John enters the barn. He looks around and
sees the body of Private Wright. He then hears
moaning coming from behind a bale of hay and
quickly goes to investigate.

A few seconds later, he finds the badly
wounded German and is visibly shocked. The
extremely weak-looking Hans smiles at him; he
then starts to shiver as he looks into his lover's
eyes. 'I am really cold'. Blood begins to spurt from
Hans' mouth as John holds his lover's hand. 'I love
you. I always have. Ever since the day we first
met'. Suddenly, he coughs and says, 'I love you ...'
He then slumps backwards and dies.

Returning to the present, John shakes his
head and states, She is totally wrong. Many Jews
fought for Germany in the Great War, and some
were heroes and were decorated. They certainly did
not have anything to do with your son's death'. He
then pauses. 'Would she really betray me, even if it
meant you being arrested?' The German nods. 'Yes,
she would. It would not bother her in the slightest.
She is utterly ruthless, and I am sorry to say,
'brainwashed'. All she thinks about is the SS. They
are her whole life now. I come a very poor second'.

John shakes his head but does not add to the conversation.

A few hours later, John and Hans look at the bed they have made in the cellar. His host glances at him. 'It is better than nothing'. He nods. 'I am truly grateful for this. One question, though'. He smiles and then queries, 'What is that?' John comes straight to the point. 'Does Gertrude ever come down into the cellar?' He shakes his head. 'No, no, never. She thinks she is too good to come down here, given that it is mostly full of cleaning materials, and I am expected to do the housework. She once told me it is beneath her, which is why I am here. Otherwise, she said that she would have 'got rid' of me years ago'. John shakes his head. 'I understand more now what you meant. She has completely changed, which is a great shame. That said, it is a great relief to me that she does not come down here; that is for sure'. Hans looks at his companion. 'No, she has not changed; you just did not notice last time you were here what she is really like'. He glances at his companion. 'I can remember her hardly talking to me when I visited Hans, but I did not think anything about it at the time'. The German nods but says nothing else.

The following week, Gertrude, dressed in her SS Uniform, checks the kitchen cupboards while her husband looks on. 'We seem to be going through a lot more food recently'. He shrugs his shoulders. 'I had not noticed, to be honest'.

Gertrude checks her watch. 'Anyway, I have to go. We will talk about it later. You better not be giving any of it away, or they will be trouble, and you will be in a camp before you can say 'Adolf Hitler', believe me. So do not take me for a fool Hans'. He ignores his wife's comment as she leaves the room.

Once he is sure she is safely out of the way, he knocks on the cellar door three times before opening it.

A few seconds later, he enters the cellar. John has a worried look on his face. 'I heard Gertrude mention the food'. He lifts his hands as if to dismiss the remark. 'Do not worry about it. It will be fine, trust me. You can come out now because she has gone for the day'.

Two days later, John's parents are sitting in easy chairs listening to Neville Chamberlain's broadcast to the nation on the radio. Mr. Chamberlain says, 'This morning, the British Ambassador in Berlin handed the German Government a final note stating that, unless we heard from them by eleven o'clock that they were prepared at once to withdraw their troops from Poland, a state of war would exist between us. I have to tell you now that no such undertaking has been received and that, consequently, this country is at war with Germany. You can imagine what a bitter blow it is to me that all my long struggle to win peace has failed. Yet I cannot believe that there is anything more or anything different that I could

have done and that would have been more successful. Up to the very last, it would have been quite possible to have arranged a peaceful and honorable settlement between Germany and Poland. But Hitler would not have it. He had evidently made up his mind to attack Poland, whatever happened, and although he now says he put forward reasonable proposals which were rejected by the Poles, that is not a true statement. The proposals were never shown to the Poles nor to us, and though they were announced in a German broadcast on
Thursday night, Hitler did not wait to hear comments on them but ordered his troops to cross the Polish frontier. His action shows convincingly that there is no chance of expecting that this man will ever give up his practice of using force to gain his will. He can only be stopped by force. We and France are today, in fulfilment of our obligations, going to the aid of Poland, who is so bravely resisting this wicked and unprovoked attack upon her people. We have a clear conscience. We have done all that any country could do to establish peace, but a situation in which no word given by Germany's ruler could be trusted and no people or country could feel themselves safe had become intolerable. And now that we have resolved to finish it, I know that you will all play your part with calmness and courage. In a moment like this, the assurances of support that we have received from the Empire are a source of profound encouragement to us. Now, may God bless you all, and may He defend the right. For it is evil things

that we shall be fighting against, brute force, bad faith, injustice, oppression and persecution. And against them, I am certain that the right will prevail'.

Harriet looks worried as her husband gets up and hugs her. 'Look, dear, John is strong. If anyone can get out of Germany, he can. Look at the courage he showed in the last war.' Just then, there is a knock at the front door. Peter gets up and leaves the room.

Within a few seconds, he opens the front door and is confronted by a little man (Tony) who is wearing a suit. Peter glares at him. 'If you are a Salesman, I am not interested'. Tony smiles. 'I am not a Salesman; I can assure you of that. But I need to speak to you and your wife about your son John'. He looks shocked, beckons Tony to enter. 'You had better come in then'.

A minute later, Tony sits on the settee and looks directly at Peter and Harriet before showing them his ID. 'Firstly, I am Tony Garbutt from MI5. I was hoping to get here before the Prime Minister's broadcast. However, despite my best efforts, I did not quite make it in time. Please accept my sincere apologies for that'. The pair are taken aback as Tony continues. 'This is going to be a shock to you both, but we recruited John to do what seemed to be a straightforward job for us in Germany'. Peter has a puzzled look on his face. 'What kind of job?' The agent shakes his head. 'I honestly cannot say anything about the reason that he was in Germany. However, he was compromised. There was contact a couple of weeks ago, but unfortunately, there has been nothing from him since'. Harriet suddenly starts to cry. Tony gives her a look of pity as he carries on with what he has to say. 'I am sorry for your distress, Mrs. Wray, but I have no reason to think that John is dead. He said that he and another operative are going to try and get out of Germany and head for Switzerland'. Peter gives him a questioning look. 'It will be much harder to achieve that now that we are at war with Germany'. He nods in agreement. 'I certainly cannot argue with you there, Mr. Wray. It goes without saying that you both will be the first to know if we hear anything regarding John'. Peter nods. 'Thank you, Tony. That means a lot to both Harriet and me'.

At the same time, Hans enters the cellar looking stern-faced. John looks at him. 'What is wrong?' He instantly reveals, 'Britain has declared war on Germany after we invaded Poland'. John's expression changes as they hear a door open upstairs. Hans panics. 'Gertrude! She must have forgotten something'. John quickly gets his pistol out from under his pillow.

Gertrude enters the kitchen and shouts,

'Hans!' There is no answer. She then mutters to herself, 'Stupid man. He is probably giving our food away again, the idiot. One of these days, I will

put him out of his misery, the horrible little man.
He is almost as bad as the Jews'.

Chapter Nine

In the meantime, back in the cellar, John looks at the panic-stricken Hans. 'Tell her that you are coming.' He then realizes that the door is still open.

Gertrude walks towards the cellar door. She notices that it is open and shouts, 'Hans. Are you down there?' From the cellar, he shouts back, 'I am coming. I was just looking for a bucket to use to wash the kitchen floor'.

A minute later, he appears from the cellar without the bucket. He also looks extremely flustered. Gertrude notices this and glares at him. 'What are you up to Hans?' He spreads his arms 'Nothing'. His wife continues to glare at him prior to yelling, 'Do not lie to me; you know where you will end up if you do. It would only take a click of my fingers, and you would be in a work camp. Do not ever forget that'. Without saying another word, she then heads towards the cellar steps.

Back in the cellar, John ensures that his pistol is loaded and points it towards the cellar door.

Gertrude looks down the flight of steps. As she starts to make her way into the cellar, Hans pushes her from behind without hesitation, and she falls down the steps and into the cellar itself.

Her head hits the stone floor. She screams out
in pain before opening her eyes and stares at John
before shouting, 'You! You dirty little Jew. I knew
something was going on with the food going
missing'.

Less than a minute later, Hans, now back in
the cellar, looks down at his wife. John stares at
him as he tries to explain his actions. 'I had to do it.
I could not risk her finding you down here'.
Gertrude moans as John asks, 'What do you want
to do Hans?' He looks at Gertrude and then at John.
'We will have to kill her. Otherwise, she will give
you away. He shakes his head. 'But she is your
wife!' 'She stopped being my wife the day she
joined the Nazi Party. Whatever happens to her
from now on, she has brought on herself'. With
that, Gertrude tries to get up.

Without any further hesitation, Hans grabs
John's pistol and shoots Gertrude in the stomach.
Her head hits the floor with a thud. She does not
move again and is obviously dead.

At that moment, John thinks back to his time
in the barn …

Private Walsh is now back in the barn loft.
Hans, who still has the pistol pointed at the
hostages, looks at him and proposes, 'As already
has been said if you let me go, no one ever needs to
know what happened'. He glances at the two
hostages and asks, 'What about those two?' Hans

smiles, and then, without warning, he shoots them both. They keel over and are clearly dead. After a few seconds, He half smiles and then states, 'Problem solved. They cannot tell anyone now because they are dead'.

Returning to the present, Hans gives John his pistol back. 'It had to be done. I had no choice'. He is taken aback as Hans looks at him 'Gertrude has treated me like dirt for years. She also told the SS about our Jewish neighbors, many of whom were my friends that I had known for years. I simply could not let her do the same thing to you'. After a few seconds, John reluctantly nods. 'Your son was the same as you. I know in my own mind that he would have done what you did today. Of that, I have no doubt'.

After they have both got over the shock of what has just happened, John spots a wooden chest in the corner of the cellar and points to it. 'We could hide her body in that?' He nods in agreement. The pair of them pause for a few seconds and then lift the chest over into the middle of the room before emptying it of the old clothes that it had contained before putting the body into it. They lift her legs up so she will fit. Hans puts the clothes on top of his wife before closing the lid. Finally, with some effort, the pair put the chest back where it originally was, covering it with an old blanket that had been stored inside. Hans then glances at his companion. 'We need to get going soon, as the SS will come looking for her once they realize that she

has not turned up for work'. 'Yes. We do not want
to be here when they arrive; that is for sure'.

Once the pair are safely up the steps and
outside the cellar door, Hans closes it, takes a key
from his trouser pocket, and locks it. He then
returns the key to his pocket before heading
towards the kitchen.

Chapter Ten

Meanwhile, at the local SS Headquarters, SS Commandant Erwin Muller is sitting at his desk. He picks up his telephone receiver and speaks to his secretary. 'Is Gertrude in yet? ... That is very unusual. She is usually here by now ... Can you send someone to her house to check on her to ensure she is alright? ... Very good. Thank you. He then replaces the receiver.

Back in the kitchen, Hans grabs some food from the cupboards and puts it into a cloth bag, which is on the kitchen table. He fails to notice that he has dropped a piece of bread (which he accidentally kicks so that it is half hidden under the cooker) onto the floor in his haste. John enters. 'We need to get moving, as we need to get as much time as we can between us and the SS'. The German nods in agreement. 'We will take Gertrude's car and dump it once we get out of Dusseldorf'. He picks up the bag as he continues. 'We are all set to go now'. John then hands him a pistol. 'It must have been Gertrude's'. 'Yes, it was. She was extremely proud of it. Not that it did her any good in the end. Anyway, it is no good looking back now'. He puts it into his belt. They both head towards the kitchen door. On his way out, Hans stops to pick up the car keys, which are on the bench.

Twenty minutes later, Hans is driving the car as the pair head out of Dusseldorf.

At the same time, an SS officer knocks on Hans' and Gertrude's door. He pauses and then knocks again. There is no answer, so he walks away, heading back towards his parked car.

Shortly after, Erwin is sitting at his desk in his office, writing a letter, when the SS officer enters. He looks up at him. 'Was Gertrude at home?' He shakes his head. 'No, Herr Commandant, she was not. There was no answer'. Erwin has a concerned look on his face. 'It is not like her not to turn up for work without letting me know'. He gets up from his desk and looks at the SS officer. 'Something is not right here. Come on, we are going back to her house now'.

Chapter Eleven

Shortly after, Erwin is hammering on Hans' and Gertrude's front door. Once again, there is no answer. He looks where Gertrude's car is usually parked, then glances at the SS officer who is with him. 'Gertrude's car has gone. Go round the back and check if you can see anything.' He nods and shouts loudly, 'Yes, Herr Commandant.' He then leaves him standing alone, looking as if he is thinking about what to do next.

The SS officer peers through the window at the back of the house. He sees nothing and is about to walk away. He then notices that a side window is open. After successfully trying, he only just manages to squeeze through the gap and scramble into the house.

In what seems like no time at all, he opens the front door. Erwin looks surprised as the SS officer explains, 'A window was left open, Herr Commandant.' He nods without adding to the conversation as he enters the house and heads straight towards the kitchen.

Erwin quickly looks around. Nothing at all looks untoward. He glances at his companion. 'Go and look around the rest of the house'. The SS officer nods and once again says loudly, 'Yes, Herr Commandant'. He then leaves Erwin, sitting deep in his own thoughts. He says to himself, 'Something is not right. I can smell a rat here'.

Shortly after, the SS officer returns to the kitchen and looks at Erwin. 'Gertrude cannot just disappear, Herr Commandant'. Just then, Erwin notices the half-hidden piece of bread on the floor, which appears to have been dropped from the cupboard. He then gets up and looks behind the door. 'As I suspected, something is not right. Every time I have been here, there has been a cloth bag behind the door. Plus, that piece of bread would not be just left there. Gertrude simply would not have allowed it. She is far too house proud for that'. The SS officer nods in agreement. 'Someone has left here in a hurry; of that there is no doubt, Herr Commandant'. Erwin looks at him. 'Also, where is Hans? He could be the key to all this. He refused to join the Nazi Party; maybe that has something to do with it, I do not know'. His fellow German nods but does not say another word. After a brief pause, the pair leave the kitchen.

Erwin stops outside the cellar door and looks at his subordinate. 'I am coming back with four men to search this house from top to bottom, as something is obviously very wrong here, and I aim to get to the bottom of it if it is the last thing I do'.

In the meantime, Hans is still driving Gertrude's car. John is in the front seat, looking at the map that had previously been in the SS officer's car, who was killed at Joe's house. He looks at his co-passenger. 'According to this, we are not far away from Frankfurt'. Hans nods as he continues. 'We will have to dump this car and steal another one when we get there'.

An hour later, back at Hans' and Gertrude's house, Erwin and four SS officers enter the kitchen. Erwin looks at them all. 'Search the house from top to bottom for clues as to where Gertrude has gone. As I said before, she cannot just disappear'. The four men leave to start their hunt. In the meantime, once again, Erwin sits at the kitchen table.

Shortly after, one of the SS officers enters the kitchen and glances at Erwin. 'We cannot find anything unusual, Herr Commandant. Nothing is out of place, nothing at all'. He nods. 'Alright, come on, follow me.'

Within a minute, the five men are outside the cellar door. Erwin tries the handle, but the door is locked. He pauses for a second, then looks at one of the officers and shouts, 'Kick it in'. He does as he is told, and after four swift kicks, the door finally bursts open. The five men hastily head down the steps, three or four at a time.

Erwin and the four officers look around the cellar. Nothing appears to be out of place as Erwin looks at his men. 'Why was the door locked? We are missing something badly wrong here. Rip this place apart'.

Ten minutes later, there is rubbish strewn all

over the floor. Erwin then notices the blanket. He goes over to it, pulls it off the chest and opens it. His face turns white as he sees Gertrude's stiffening corpse. He shouts loudly, 'Hans! You bastard, I will get you for this if it is the last thing I do'.

Chapter Twelve

At precisely the same time, John is driving a different car. Hans is in the passenger seat. John glances at his friend. 'Well, stealing this car was easy. We will have to get rid of it when we get to Stuttgart and grab another.' He nods. 'I agree we need to keep one step ahead of the SS'. He pauses for a few seconds. Do you want to pull over for something to eat?' John smiles. 'That sounds like a good idea'.

Meanwhile, Erwin is sitting at his desk. He asks himself out loud. 'Why would Hans kill his wife? What is he up to?' He pauses for thought for a few seconds and then adds, 'We need to find their car. That is probably the key to all of this'. He picks up his telephone receiver.

A few hours later, an SS officer is walking down a street and finds Gertrude's abandoned car. He is on the outskirts of Frankfurt.

Shortly after, Erwin's phone rings. He picks up the receiver and states, 'Frankfurt? ... That is very odd ... Leave the car where it is. I will be there as soon as I can'. He gets up from his seat, stops at the coat stand, puts on his coat, and then heads towards the door. He leaves and closes the aforementioned door behind him.

Much later in the day, Erwin's car stops

behind Gertrude's.

Back with John and Hans, Hans looks in the food bag. 'There is not much left to eat in here'. His companion, who is now driving, glances at him before quickly turning his attention back to the road. 'We need to get some more provisions, as we have not got enough left to last us until we get to the Swiss border'. 'We could break into a house and steal some'. John gives him a questioning look. 'That would be risky'. He half smiles. 'Hopefully, no one will be there when we do it'. John nods. 'Yes, I agree. That would certainly help'.

Back where Gertrude's car was found, Erwin is sitting in the driver's seat of her car. Again, he thinks out loud and asks himself, 'Why would he leave the car? What is he up to? That is what I need to find out'.

A few hours later, John stops outside an isolated house. His companion gets out and heads up the path that leads to the building.

Within two minutes, he knocks on the front door. Shortly after, the door opens, and he is confronted by an SS officer. He looks at him sternly. 'What do you want?' Hans smiles. 'My car has overheated. I was wondering whether I could have some water?' His fellow German nods. 'I suppose so. Come in'. Hans steps into the passageway. The SS officer looks at him. 'Wait there, I will be back in a minute'. He heads towards the kitchen. Once he is out of sight, Hans gets his pistol out from inside his jacket pocket and waits for the owner of the house to return.

A little later, the SS officer comes out with a jug of water. Before he can do anything, Hans shoots him in the stomach three times. He drops to the floor and remains still. The jug crashes to the floor, spilling the water in the process.

Once he gets over killing a man in cold blood, he looks around the passageway and quickly notices a cloth bag; he grabs it without even looking inside and then puts it into his jacket pocket.

He leaves and heads upstairs. Shortly after, he quickly looks into the downstairs rooms.

On his return, he enters the kitchen, goes through the cupboards, and takes several tins of meat. He puts them in his coat before leaving the house, just as he did when he entered.

Thirty seconds later, John sees his cohort approaching.

A minute later, a visibly shaken Hans gets into the car. John looks at him. 'Are you alright?' He nods before revealing, 'I killed the SS officer who was in the house'. 'What the hell have I got you into?' He glances at his passenger. 'Look, we are in this together, so that is the end of that talk. If

I didn't want to be here, I wouldn't be. It is as simple as that. You did not force me to come with you'. John smiles. 'I still feel bad for bringing all this trouble to your door'. Hans looks directly at him. 'As I said, I am here because I want to be; I also know that if he were here, my son would be doing exactly the same thing; he would be by your side in place of me. I know that one hundred per cent. With that in mind, I will do everything possible to help us both reach Switzerland. Nothing will stop me from doing that unless I am killed trying'. John briefly touches his companion's arm. 'I am glad that you are here with me; your son would be very proud of you; I know that for sure'. John pauses for a few seconds and then continues. 'Anyway, was there anyone else in the house?' He shakes his head. 'No. I checked the whole place. He must have lived there alone, as there were no women's or children's things in any of the rooms'.

Shortly after, both men enter the passageway of the now-dead SS officer's house. John looks at the body and pauses. He then glances at his companion and suggests, 'We should take the body with us and get rid of it somewhere secluded, where hopefully, it will not be found for quite a while'. He nods in agreement. 'Good idea. I will go and look for some weapons before we leave'.

Chapter Thirteen

Ten minutes later, Hans, now with a machine gun over his shoulder, helps John pick the body up. Then they head towards the door.

Shortly after, the pair dump the corpse of the SS officer into a ditch and cover it up with leaves and branches. John glances at the German before saying, 'Hopefully, by the time he is discovered, if he ever is, we will be in Switzerland'. 'We have hidden him well enough; there is not a lot more that we can do to be honest'.

At around the same time, Erwin is sitting at his desk reading a file. The SS officer enters and looks at him. 'Herr Commandant, there is a British spy on the loose in Germany. We are sure that he has something to do with Gertrude's death'. Erwin has a surprised look on his face. 'How do you come to that conclusion, soldier? I am extremely interested to know'. He glances at his commanding officer before continuing. 'Two SS officers were killed in Berlin; their car was stolen and was found hidden in some undergrowth just outside Dusseldorf'. Erwin shakes his head. 'You have totally lost me. I still do not see the connection at all'. His comrade once again continues. 'Hans and Gertrude's neighbors were interviewed. They admitted that they had known an Englishman named John Wray for years; we now know that John Wray is a British spy. He looks at the SS officer questioningly. 'How do we know that it is definitely him?' He smiles. 'Because one of our double agents warned us that a British spy named John Wray was coming to Germany, posing as a journalist. So far, he has managed to elude capture. However, two other British spies, named Paul and Joe, together with five of our SS officers, have been found dead at two different addresses in Berlin'. Erwin pauses to think before asking himself, 'I wonder where he is now? He is probably trying to get out of Germany'. He ponders for a few seconds and then exclaims, 'Switzerland!' He then looks at his subordinate before continuing. 'Alert the border guards. Additionally, arrange for all trains and cars heading to Switzerland to undergo thorough checks. I do not want even a mouse to get through'. He salutes Erwin and then shouts, 'Yes, Herr Commandant. I will do exactly as you have ordered'. He then salutes Erwin before leaving the room.

Erwin pauses and then says to himself, 'Perhaps I underestimated this situation and, more importantly, this John Wray character completely'.

Chapter Fourteen

In the meantime, Hans is driving the car. John is half asleep in the passenger seat. The German looks at the fuel gauge and then nudges him. 'We are getting very low on petrol'. He smirks. 'No problem. We will have another car soon, so I would not worry about it. We have enough to get us to Stuttgart, which is the main thing'.

Later that evening, Hans is walking down a Stuttgart street looking for a car to steal. He tries a vehicle door, but it is locked. He then goes to the next one in the row. The door is open, so he gets in. Just then, a Hitler Youth Boy knocks on the window. 'Is this your car?' Hans nods as the Hitler Youth boy continues. 'But I saw you try the other car door first. Can you get out of the vehicle?' Hans gets his pistol from his belt. He then gets out of the car and, without hesitation, shoots the Hitler Youth Boy, just before he blows his whistle. He falls to the ground and remains motionless. A few seconds later, he opens the back door of the car before quickly dragging the boys' lifeless body into the back seat.

Hans stops the car on the outskirts of Stuttgart. He lifts the boy's body out of the car and hides it in the undergrowth, ensuring that it cannot be seen. He then looks where it is now hidden. 'I am very sorry, young man, but you should not have gone for your whistle. Then, I would not have had to kill you. I hope that God forgives me when my time comes to enter heaven, if I do end up there, that is'.

The following day, Hans is driving the car. He glances at John. 'I still feel bad for killing that boy. I cannot get it out of my mind'. 'You had no choice. If he had blown his whistle, you would have been captured or even killed'. Hans nods. 'I realize that, but funnily enough, as you probably know, I do not feel guilty at all about killing Gertrude. She was evil, and in my opinion, she deserved it'. His co-passenger ends the conversation by remarking, 'The difference is that it was a young boy. But what you need to remember is that, like Gertrude, he was brainwashed, so in real terms, they are exactly the same'. He nods in partial agreement but does not say another word.

A few minutes later, John spots a sign that says 'Konstanz 90 KM'. He looks at Hans. 'When we arrive where we need to be, we will leave the car somewhere out of sight, wait until it is dark, then we will try and get across the border.' He nods and then looks at him. 'I think we are being followed'. John glances at his fellow passenger. 'Slow down; hopefully, the car behind will pass us'. The German does as he is asked. The driver of the car behind does precisely the same thing. Without hesitation, John grabs the machine gun from near his feet and loads it. Hans looks behind.

'There are two men in the car that is following us'.
John climbs into the back seat. He smashes the back
window with the machine gun and fires at the car.
Its front left tire is hit. The car swerves off the road,
crashes into a tree, and then bursts into flames. John
looks at Hans and then confirms, 'I hit one of the
tires. He breathes a sigh of relief. 'Thank God for
that. But now, the only thing is we will need to take
the longer route to Konstanz via more secluded
roads because we now know for certain that they
are looking for us'.

Chapter Fifteen

Later that day, the SS officer enters Erwin's office. He looks at his commanding officer, who is sitting at his desk. 'Herr Commandant, one of our officers was murdered in the countryside, and then later, a Hitler Youth boy was killed in Stuttgart. Their bodies were both found hidden in undergrowth near to where they met their end. The SS officer's house had been ransacked, and food was taken'. He shakes his head. 'It must be them. It simply has to be. Have we had any luck with the vehicle stolen in Stuttgart?' The SS officer shakes his head as Erwin continues. I will get them if it is the last thing I do'.

A few hours later, Hans is walking up a side street in Singen. He notices a parked car. He looks around before trying the driver's side door, which he quickly discovers is open. Without incident, he jumps in, starts the car, and quickly drives away.

Shortly after, Hans is driving the car. As per usual, John is in the passenger seat. Hans glances at his cohort. 'We will leave the car in Hilzingen and then walk across the border'. He nods. 'They will be waiting for us, you know that, don't you?' The German quickly glances at him but does not utter a single word.

Several hours later, Hans pulls over near a wooded area just outside Hilzingen. After pausing for a few seconds, he drives the car away from the road and stops where it cannot be seen. John glances at him. 'We will stay here until it is dark. Then we will try to get across the border. 'Good idea. We might have a better chance if we try then'.

In the meantime, Erwin is sitting at his desk reading a file when his telephone rings. He picks up the receiver. 'Singen? ... Smashed back window ... Dead? ... Why haven't we caught them? ... Between them, they have left a trail of dead bodies right across Germany ... They are heading for the border ... At all costs, do not let them get away'. After he has finished the conversation, he slams the telephone down and bangs the desk with his fist. He then gets up, walks over to where his coat is hung, retrieves it, and puts it on. He then leaves his office. In his haste, he does not close the door behind him, as is usually the case.

Back at the car, Hans looks at his fellow passenger. 'I forgot to tell you earlier; I picked up a bag from the SS officer's house. It is in the boot'. He looks intrigued. 'What is in it?' Hans shrugs his shoulders. 'With everything that was going on, I did not get the chance to look. Then I forgot about it until now'.

A minute later, Hans opens the car boot, removes the bag, and places his hand in it. He pulls

out three German hand grenades. John, who is
standing beside him, looks surprised. 'Is there

anything else in it?' His companion pulls out
another pistol and some ammunition. John smiles as
he continues. 'They will all come in handy.' Hans
puts the items back in the bag and has them with
him as the pair get back into the car.

Shortly after, the pair are sitting in the car.
John looks at his friend. 'I have been thinking,
maybe we should use the car to get over the
border'. He seems to be in thought as John
continues. 'We will slow down near the border
point, throw the grenades out of the window and
then open fire with the machine gun. Hopefully, we
will kill all of the guards'. He nods without saying a
single word.

Chapter Sixteen

Under the cover of darkness, John drives the car towards the border crossing. Hans ensures the grenades are ready, the pistols and machine guns are properly loaded, and the safety catches are off. John glances at his companion. 'We are not far from the border crossing now.' He nods and then picks up one of the pistols and puts it between his legs.

Less than a minute later, John points ahead. 'The border point is coming up'. As he slows down, a German soldier holds up his hand as he sees a car approaching. John stops the car. Before the soldier can do anything, Hans shoots him in the stomach. The soldier drops to the ground, does not move and is clearly dead. Hans then spots two more soldiers running out of the guard hut. He throws a hand grenade in their direction, and then, to complete the job, he shoots them both. They drop to the ground, and once again, they are motionless. Within a few seconds, the hand grenade goes off, and it blows the hut to pieces. Without hesitation, John drives off at speed.

At the same time, a German soldier stumbles from where the hut was and aims his machine gun at the fleeing car and fires. He then falls down as he is, without doubt, badly wounded.
Unfortunately, Hans is hit in the back and slumps forward. Looking concerned, John glances at his co-

passenger and shouts, 'Hold on, Hans. We are almost there, my friend'.

A Swiss soldier sees a car speeding towards him and holds up his hand. John sees him and slows down. The car stops next to him, and he gets out. He looks at the soldier. 'I take it that we are in Switzerland?' He nods but says nothing as John continues. 'Thank God for that. Do you have a medic here? My friend has been shot'. He shakes his head. 'No. But we have a First Aid Kit. I will go and get it for you'. He then turns away from him and runs towards the guard hut. John then gets out of the car and opens the passenger door.

A weakened Hans looks at his friend and states, 'We made it, John'. He then starts to shiver. 'I am cold'. Blood begins to spurt from his mouth, and within a few seconds, he slumps in his seat and dies.

Without warning and not for the first time, John thinks back to his final moments with his former lover…

John enters the barn. He looks around and sees the body of Private Wright. He then hears moaning coming from behind a bale of hay and quickly goes to investigate.

A few seconds later, he finds the badly wounded German and is visibly shocked. The extremely weak-looking Hans smiles at him; he then starts to shiver as he looks into his lover's eyes. 'I am really cold'. Blood begins to spurt from Hans' mouth as John holds his lover's hand. 'I love you. I always have. Ever since the day we first met'. Suddenly, he coughs and says, 'I love you ...' He then slumps backwards and dies.

Returning to the present day, a jeep stops on the German side of the border (this brings John out of his deep thoughts). Erwin and the SS officer get out. Now holding a First Aid Kit, the Swiss soldier looks at Erwin. 'You cannot come any further. You know that, don't you?' He nods. 'Do not worry; I have no intention of entering your country as I do not have the authority to do so'. 'As long as you understand that, soldier'. Erwin smiles. 'I promise you, there will not be a diplomatic incident here today. You have my word on that'.

John then looks the German straight in the eye from the Swiss side of the border. Thanks to my German friend, who is now dead, I am safe from you'. Erwin smiles again. 'I have to say, you both proved very elusive to catch. I must congratulate you on that. Not many people can say that they have beaten the whole of the German SS. But you can honestly say that you did'. John shrugs his shoulders in the Commandant's direction. 'That was the last thing on my mind. Now, I have a couple of things to say. Firstly, I am sorry for having to kill so many of your people in order to escape. It is the last thing I wanted to do'. The German half-smiles. 'These things happen in war and when people are desperate, unfortunately'. John nods. 'Even so, it is not something that I enjoyed'. Erwin pauses for a couple of seconds. 'And the second thing you wanted to say?' Like Erwin, John also pauses. 'I honestly think that our two countries could learn a lot from Hans' family. I have known him since before the First World War, which his son, also called Hans and I fought in. I helped him then, when we got into a situation, I was going to let him go rather than take him prisoner. Unfortunately, despite my best efforts, he was killed. And now, almost twenty years later, his father did everything he could to get me out of Germany, at the cost of his own life'. He nods as the SS officer gets his pistol from its holster and points it at John. He is about to shoot. Erwin notices just in time and shouts, 'No!' He then knocks the SS officer's arm. There is a shot that goes into the air. He then glares at his fellow German and yells, 'Put that away. At once'. He hesitates before lowering his weapon. Erwin continues to glare at him and shouts, 'Get back into the jeep, now'. He turns and does as he is told. Erwin then smiles at John. 'I am really sorry about that. He has no morals'. He pauses before continuing. 'Thinking about what you said, you could be right. Maybe we could all learn from your story. Who knows? Perhaps, no one ever will. I certainly hope so, though'. He then smiles once more before turning and heading towards his jeep. He suddenly stops and says, 'Good luck'. He then continues his journey, leaving a forlorn-looking John standing with the Swiss Border Guard.

Meanwhile, several jeeps pull up on the German side of the border. Erwin glances at the driver of the lead vehicle. 'Turn around. Everything is sorted. We have nothing else to do here. Let's go home'.

Acknowledgements

Firstly, a huge 'thank you' must go to my wife, Jennifer, for her unwavering patience, and to my PA, Chris, for his constant practical support.

Next, I would like to express my gratitude to the actor and my friend, Bill Fellows, for writing the foreword to this book. I have known Bill for many years. For those of you who do not know, Bill played the role of my father (Norman) in the feature film Give Them Wings, which is loosely based on my life story. That aside, no one was happier than I when he was cast in Coronation Street as 'Stu', a role he played to perfection!

In addition, I would also like to thank four special friends, especially Ian Carter, Stephen Lowson, Roger Martin, and John Gray, for their ongoing support as I continue on my writing journey.

I want to show my appreciation to the following ex-Darlington players (and a few former managers) who, through playing for the club, have become firm friends: Mark Forster, Kevan Smith, David Speedie, Neil Wainwright, Jimmy Willis, Andy Toman, Alan Walsh, Roger Wicks, Jarrett Rivers, Peter Kirkham, Craig Liddle, Adam Reed, David Hodgson, Brian Little, Jack Winstanley, Ciaran Dixon, Paul Ward and Dale Anderson. All of them have been a massive support to me over the years. Here is one comment regarding most of these lads. I have known the vast majority of them for many years, and they have always tried to support me in whatever I decide to do at any particular time. I am grateful for this and never take their support for granted.

Last but not least, I am incredibly grateful to current Darlington FC CEO David Johnston for his help and support with this and the many other projects I have undertaken since we met back in 2019. The same can be said of Andy Scullion and Ray Simpson, who are both heavily involved in the football club I am passionate about.

About the Author

Paul's first venture into writing occurred in the late 1990s, when he began collaborating with a co-writer on his first work, 'Flipper's Side' (his life story). It was published in 2000 and has been out of print for some time.

His second book was titled 'When Push Comes to Shove', the story of two seasons of him and several friends following Darlington FC up and down the country and what happened to him during these trips. Paul openly admits that this work is not his best (in his opinion); however, he enjoyed collating all the required information to assemble it over the two years it took. Despite the project not being one of his favorites, to his surprise, it sold out once again. He once said to his friend Ian Carter, 'It just goes to show, despite me not being keen on the end product, the Darlington fans absolutely loved it. Maybe I was a tad harsh on myself, who knows?' Even though the book sold out, as mentioned above, all these years later, he maintains that it is his least favorite work he has ever written.

Paul completed his third book, 'Give Them Wings,' in 2021. The book is a significantly expanded version of 'Flipper's Side' and updates his life from 2000 to 2020.

Interestingly, whilst the film of the same

name is not based on the book, some of the stories were taken from it. The film was based on 'Flipper's Side', as per Paul's wish.

The following year, his next work, 'One Hundred of the Best', which details Paul's favorite one hundred Darlington FC games, was released and went down really well with 'Quakers' fans. Unlike 'When Push Comes to Shove', his previous work about Darlington FC, Paul is proud of this work, his first published by Pitch Publishing, whom he thinks very highly of.

Paul is also an accomplished scriptwriter. He is exceptionally proud of his over 100 writing awards (all IMDb-recognized).

One of those scripts, 'Give Them Wings', as mentioned above, was released as a film to great acclaim in July 2022 and has since been distributed worldwide, currently doing extremely well, which is brilliant news and very pleasing for all concerned in the project.

Several well-known actors appeared in the film, including singer Toyah Willcox, who played his mother, and former Coronation Street Star Bill Fellows, who played his father, as mentioned earlier. Over the years, Bill, in particular, has been highly proactive in promoting Paul and his projects, as have several other cast members. This demonstrates the high regard in which he is held in the film industry.

Paul has also written several other screenplays, which people in the film business are intensely interested in. These are 'John's Journey', 'John's Journey Two' (this book is based on them both) and 'The Hill'. He also recently finished writing a seven-part TV series called 'Ryker' with the Artistic Assistance of Actor Johnny Farrell and his wife, Jennifer, which he is incredibly excited about. The trio knew in their own minds that 'Ryker' would be loved by television audiences. It's just a matter of getting it out there; that's the challenge for the threesome and any other aspiring film or television writers.

In addition to 'One Hundred of the Best' (which has already been discussed above), 'For the Love of Darlo', which details Paul's early life, was released in August 2024 and reached the top one hundred best sellers on Amazon, which was very pleasing for both the publisher and Paul himself.

In many ways, this book is a prequel to both 'Flippers Side' and 'Give Them Wings'. Paul openly admits that he found this book extremely difficult to write because it brought aspects of his life to the forefront that he purposely left out of the other books. After all, he did not feel ready to disclose them until then.

Now, he feels that everything he wanted to say has been said, and his biography series is complete. Therefore, after 24 years and three books, he can move on. The task is now complete in his mind, and nothing else will be written about his life unless anything extraordinary happens to him in the coming years.

In January 2025, 'Another One Hundred of the Best was released. The author reveals one hundred Darlington players who have played for the club in his lifetime and have stuck in his mind for many reasons. Paul feels he has one more Darlington FC-based book left in him; this will also spell the end of that series. Once again, he enjoyed doing the research and, indeed, writing this book.

Additionally, 'The David Speedie Story', which chronicles the football legend's life and career, is scheduled for publication later this year (2025). Both Paul and David are incredibly pleased with how this project has turned out and are sure that football fans from all clubs will enjoy it.

Aside from writing, Paul enjoys following Darlington Football Club when he can and researching his family history, which he has worked on and off for over 20 years with his best friend, Ian Carter.

At the time of writing, he has almost 20,000 names on his family tree. They are all blood relatives, something that, once again, he is extremely proud of. He has one ambition concerning this remaining. Paul wants to find out who his five-time great-grandfather is. The pair of them (Ian and Paul) are determined to resolve this mystery before Paul finally die.

AWARDS